Praise for **Shortcut Man** by p. g. sturges

"This is an assured and diverting performance, with an ending that should impress even the most seasoned fan of hardboiled detective stories. You thought every twist ending in the noir bag had been taken out and used up, p.g. sturges seems to be saying as the book rushes toward its final page. Well, get a load of this."

—*The Washington Post*

"*Shortcut Man* joins the wisecracking, bone-breaking tradition of California noir stretching from Chandler to Hammett to Robert Crais's latest Elvis Cole novel. . . . A gripping read."

—*The Boston Globe*

"I was hooked on his quirky characters and original plot turns. By the spectacularly unexpected conclusion, I was floored. Now I can hardly wait for the second installment. . . . Mr. Sturges's writing is flip and hip, influenced by a line of predecessors from Raymond Chandler to Elmore Leonard, but the unconventional writer adds a sassy cynicism of his own."

—*Pittsburgh Post-Gazette*

"*Shortcut Man* is a glorious read: powerful, clever, suspenseful, and filled with enough dark humor and shady characters to satisfy the most rabid noir fan, and convert those who aren't already."

—Associated Press

"I started laughing by page five. . . . Although Sturges stays within Raymond Chandler's noir template, his PI Dick Henry and a caravan of sociopaths kept surprising me."

—*The Kansas City Star*

Also by p. g. sturges

Tribulations of the Shortcut Man

SHORTCUT MAN

a novel

p. g. sturges

SCRIBNER

New York   London   Toronto   Sydney   New Delhi

SCRIBNER
A Division of Simon & Schuster, Inc.
1230 Avenue of the Americas
New York, NY 10020

First Scribner trade paperback edition December 2011

SCRIBNER and design are registered trademarks of The Gale Group,
Inc. used under license by Simon & Schuster, Inc., the publisher of this work.

For information about special discounts for bulk purchases,
please contact Simon & Schuster Special Sales at 1-866-506-1949
or business@simonandschuster.com.

The Simon & Schuster Speakers Bureau can bring authors to your live event. For more
information or to book an event contact the Simon & Schuster Speakers Bureau at
1-866-248-3049 or visit our website at www.simonspeakers.com.

Manufactured in the United States of America

1   3   5   7 .9   10   8   6   4   2

Library of Congress Control Number: 2010017583

ISBN 978-1-4391-9417-1
ISBN 978-1-4391-9419-5 (pbk)
ISBN 978-1-4391-9420-1 (ebook)

To Gina, my late wife, who gave me the idea for this book.
God bless thee..

To Mac and Kelly, who believed in their father.

To Sandy, my mother, who believed in her son.
And loved him enormously.

To Tom, my brother, on my side from day one.

To my father, Preston, who inspires me every day,
who gave me a ticket to the game.

To the Nagles, to the Halls,
who encouraged me in all things, always.

To author and friend R. C. Matheson, who suggested I write.

To author and friend Craig Spector, who suggested I write.

To Andy Rigrod, Paul Pompian, Dan Cartwright,
Rick Harper, Robert Barrere, Jason McKean, Diane Mullen,
and Dr. Ronald Clarke, true friends and believers.

A Note from the Author

It is not the author's intention to amend, emend, reduce, ameliorate, or redress any wrongs, misfortunes, tragedies, or perditious conditions known to exist in this world or the next. You will depart the premises no wiser than you arrived. However, it is hoped you will be entertained in the meantime.

p.g.sturges

Contents

CONTENTS

CONTENTS

PART THREE

The Business at Hand

PART ONE

Two Sides
to Every Story

CHAPTER ONE

Tisdale Regrets

Tisdale was a professional nonpayer of rent and I'd been sent to see about him. He lived in a court up off Hollywood Boulevard on Hobart.

A professional nonpayer paid his deposit, his first and last, a few more months to establish his bona fides, then settled in for a spell of hard luck.

It had come down to this, he would declare, choking a sob, his mother's medicine or the rent.

Just this once slid into twice and after a while his mother died again. By then the landlord knew he was in for a porking but too late. The nonpayer would claim hardship and file for bankruptcy. In like a tick, it could take two years and lots of money to get him out. Sometimes ten grand in legal fees alone. That's when a heads-up landlord would call me.

I'm Dick Henry. The Shortcut Man.

Tisdale's place was in the back, in the middle. The lawn on either side of the cracked concrete walk was weedy and unkempt. A few scraggly bushes surrounded one of those towering Hollywood palms whose image had lured millions to false paradise.

Meanwhile, someone nearby was torturing a guitar Van Halen style, and when I got closer it was coming from Tisdale's.

I stepped up on the little porch. I knocked through the screen and waited. The guitar quieted, someone rumbled across the floor, and the door opened.

I didn't like him right off. Approaching three hundred doughy pounds and six feet tall, red rat eyes peered through long stringy hair. The face was fat and dirty, and gave evidence of recent rib eating. I smelled cheap marijuana.

"Yeah?" said Rib Face.

I waved. "I'm Dick Henry." I tried to be pleasant.

"Yeah?"

"You Mr. Pissdale?"

"It's *Tis*-dale. With a *T*. And if you're here about my guitar, you can split right now. 'Cause I don't turn it down for nobody. I know my rights."

These guys always knew their rights. I felt a tingle in my fist.

"Actually, I don't give a shit about your guitar." I was still trying to be pleasant. "I'm here about the rent."

The concept of rent took an appreciable amount of time to make its way through the circuits. Finally it arrived.

"The rent? The *rent*? You should know better than to harass me here, fuckhead. *I* know my rights, *Landers* knows my rights, and *you* know my rights."

Tisdale ran his fingers back through his hair. "You don't come to Landers's freezy drafty leaky piece-of-shit house when I've declared bankruptcy." His teeth were a yellowish green. "Now should I call my lawyer?"

It was an option.

But by this time the tingle in my fist had turned into a buzz and suddenly it was drawn, as if by a celestial karma vacuum, right through the fly-specked screen and directly into Tisdale's nose. There was a satisfying crunch and down went Tisdale.

I pulled the door open and went in. The sight of his own blood had weakened his resolve and reorganized his priorities. I grabbed him by the collar, helped him to his feet.

"Your rights have come to an end, friend, and your obligations have begun." I checked my watch. "You got twenty-five minutes to get everything you own out of this house."

Tisdale held up a cautionary hand, eyes watering. "My nose, man. You broke my fucking nose."

I checked my watch again. "Now you've got twenty-four minutes to get out."

Tisdale attended his nose with a grayish T-shirt that had been lying around. Now it was red. Soon it would be brown. "Hey," he resumed, "you just can't throw someone out on their ass. There're laws."

In principle I agreed. In principle. "Yeah, there are laws, but they don't apply to you anymore." According to my preliminary investigation, his mother had died five times. Three times of cancer, twice of tuberculosis, once of intestinal blockage. Wait a second. That made six. And his father. A cerebral hemorrhage. And kidney failure.

There was a knock at the door. I checked my watch. It should have been Rojas.

It was.

Rojas exuded menace like a whore exudes cheap perfume. Of medium height, stocky, tattooed, unsmiling, with eyes concealed by Wayfarers under a black leather porkpie hat, Rojas was a badass Eastsider. We shook hands and a hint of a grin played in and around his soul patch.

I introduced the parties. "Enrique Rojas, meet Michael Tisdale, a.k.a. Mike Jones, Mike Smith, Mike Bush, and Mike Lane."

Tisdale searched Rojas's face for mercy.

"Buenas tardes, motherfucker," said Rojas.

Tisdale looked back at me. I hooked a thumb at friend Rojas. "Mr. Rojas is here to see that you don't backslide on your promise to vacate the premises. Otherwise I've asked him to beat the piss out of you."

"My promise to vacate?"

I checked my watch again. "You got twenty minutes."

"Hold on, man. I can't get everything out in twenty minutes. Look at this place!"

I shrugged. "Save what's most important. The rest is going in the Dumpster."

"I'm going to call the police."

"Go right ahead. I bet you have lots of friends down there."

Tisdale's only recourse was the practical. "I *can't* move out of here in twenty minutes, dude. It can't be done."

I looked at Rojas. "Mr. Tisdale says it can't be done."

Rojas nodded, looked around. Then he walked over, grabbed the TV, lugged it, connecting wires and all, out the door and dumped it over the railing. In the house, various items crashed off shelves and slouched toward Bethlehem.

"What's next?" Rojas brushed his hands upon his return.

"Start with the guitar."

Tisdale interceded with a shriek. "Please. *Please.*"

Now you get the gist of how I saved Mr. Landers $7,500. And earned $2,500 for myself. I'm Dick Henry. The Shortcut Man.

CHAPTER TWO

The Inciting Incident

My career as a shortcut man began with an unremarkable incident when I was twenty-two years old. I was a submarine sailor stationed in Hawaii, at Pearl, living in the barracks.

Returning to Pearl after a quick undersea jaunt around the islands to earn a few bigwig officers sea pay, I set off to see Nita. Nita was a full-figured Oklahoma girl, recently divorced from a soldier at Schofield. She was not going to be pretty later in life, but for the moment she glowed with the attractiveness and vivacity of any young creature. She worked nights at a coffee shop in Pearl City and was the object of my most tender feelings. Unrequited, of course.

But Nita was not in the cards that night. My car had been rendered immobile; my gearshift with the T-grip had been detached and removed. Stolen. I looked at a hole in the floor.

Angrily I marched over to Subase Security and reported the violation. Predictably, like minions of justice anywhere in the world, the night crew at security had no particular interest in justice and quickly deflected it by procedure. Did I have my social security number etched on the missing item?

What? Etched on my gearshift? Are you kidding? No.

No? Oh, well. Their hands were tied.

In lieu of action, their action, I was informed that I could fill out three copies of a long, complicated report that would sit in a drawer till somebody said what the fuck is this and round-filed it.

The next day, asking friends on other boats (submarines are called boats by those who sail on them) who might be a likely thief, I was told about Stevens. I looked into his car and there, *bingo,* installed, was my gearshift.

Again I made the trek to Subase Security, this time to inform the day shift what I had discovered. The day shift looked a lot more intelligent than the night crew. The duty chief solemnly stroked his chin, looked up at the fan. I was filled with warm, precoital gratitude. Then he inquired if I had etched my social security number on the missing item.

Down to my last legal card, I went to the captain of my boat, explained the problem. As the commander of an autonomous nuclear weapons platform, one of the most feared pillars of the free world, I had full confidence he might part the Red Sea. The captain stroked his chin, made his recommendation: go see Subase Security.

The vote was in. It was me or nobody.

I assessed myself in the mirror. I was tall and thin but strong. Steady blue eyes, wide-set, stared out from beneath red hair going brown. Freckles, the plague of my youth, were fading, though a few were still splashed across my nose, bridged and slightly crooked. When I smiled I revealed the full set of teeth God had given me, in their original, imperfect orientation. Altogether, it was not a face that launched a thousand ships. But it was not the face of a coward.

That afternoon, having borrowed a piece of bar stock from the engine room, I confronted Stevens in his room at the barracks. I knocked on his door with my iron bar.

"My gearshift is installed in your car and I want it now," I explained after he opened up.

He didn't know what I was talking about.

I slammed the bar down on the steel railing outside his door and it made a big noise. "My gearshift is installed in your car and I want it now," I repeated.

From his face, I could see that Stevens now shared my concern, but, interpreting the spread of his hands, he remained ignorant as to the cause of the misfortune.

"My gearshift is installed in your car and I want it now," I shouted. I waggled the bar like a baseball bat.

In that moment, Stevens realized he had been ripped off at the swap meet. He offered to reinstall it on the spot.

And Nita? Nita never did come my way.

CHAPTER THREE

Lynette

Hell with Nita. Now I had Lynette.

Lynette was a tantalizing witch with the face of an angel. She was whip-smart, streetwise, and had a mocking laugh that sent primordial forces straight to my cock. Coal black hair coursed down around rosebud lips and terminated at her full bosom with small, upturned, brown nipples. Part of me knew I wouldn't have her long. That was what made the living tragedy so sweet.

I met her at the Sunset Strip House of Blues, upstairs in the Founders Room after a Little Feat show. I don't know how she picked me to talk to, but perhaps I was the only one content not to be a famous musician.

"You don't play *anything*?" she inquired, pretending to be disappointed.

Her beauty might have intimidated me but the lighting was dim and I was two Laphroaigs on the good side. Earlier that day I had folded away a neat little check for $22,000. So I was feeling my oats, as they say. "I can play the swinette, in an emergency, but I know how to eat pussy."

"You're on, sailor boy," she replied with a grin.

Later she asked me what a swinette was.

"That would be three hairs across a pig's ass, but I wouldn't recommend it." It was a bad joke, but the ship had already sailed, if you get my drift.

We established a true adult relationship. She did her thing, I did mine. It was fast, it was fun. We fucked, we talked, we cooked, we laughed, we fucked. We saw little daylight but plenty of stars.

She was a stewardess for a private airline that flew billionaires wherever they needed to go to exploit natives. She would be in town for a few days, then gone for a few weeks, then, there she'd be at my door at one in the morning smoking a joint.

"What don't I have?" she asked that night with a twisty smile.

I looked her up and down. Honesty sprang to my lips and I let it pass. "You have everything."

Another devilish smile. "You're wrong, Dick. I don't have any underwear."

And we'd be off and running.

The only problem with the beautiful bitch was that she had no respect for anything or anybody. "I'll be over in fifteen minutes" could mean an hour, three hours, or not at all. And regardless of if and when, she knew no one could look into those green eyes and hold on to anger. I never could.

I was steaming this second. Of course, she was way late. I was thinking I should've gone to Las Brisas in Redondo with Rojas and had some tacos carnitas, a few Pacificos, and a few laughs.

Then I heard a knock at the door. Even her knock was feminine, don't ask me how I could tell.

There she was, smoking a joint, twirling her car keys around her finger. Then she walked in, right past me.

"What's up, Dick Henry?"

"You're lucky I'm still here."

"I'm the lucky type, sailor boy." She laughed. "I stopped and had a drink."

"Or three. You're two and a half hours late."

"Who's counting?"

"I am."

"I'm not late, Dick. I *can't* be late."

"How's that?"

"Because the party starts when I get here, darling."

With that I grinned and gave up.

She reached the mantelpiece and paused to reexamine a small abstract sculpture.

The piece was the size of an abalone shell, but there were extra rolls, flourishes, and cavities. In kiln-fired red, purple, and green. Maybe it was an alien vagina. To greet the three-headed cocks of Orlanafon.

"What did you say this was, again, Dick?"

"A piece an ex-client made for me. And hello, by the way."

She prodded it with a finger. "In lieu of payment, no doubt."

Uhh, that was true. "I can't remember."

"Everyone takes you to the cleaners." She pushed it to the edge just to see if I'd react. I didn't.

Then she pushed it off. It shattered on the flat of the fireplace.

"God*damm*it. Why'd you do that?" I didn't know what it was, but it was mine.

She laughed. "Try to surround yourself with objects of beauty, Dick. It matters. It really does."

Then she walked over, theatrically put her head on my chest, looked up into my eyes, batted her eyelashes. "You're not really mad at me, are you, darling? Not for that."

What I was, was in over my head.

She relit the joint. "Let's go to Big Sur."

A friend of hers had a house there, and we'd driven up once.

She'd treated the place like she owned it. Incredible view from a cliff above the ocean, a huge bed, nice liquor cabinet. But tonight, too far.

I fought my way out of her game. "You're drunk."

"I'm illuminated."

"What's the difference?" There was brilliant riposte.

"Intent."

"And what do you intend?"

"I want to fuck."

Point, set, overmatched. I exhaled slowly. "Turn around."

I saw the pulse in her throat. Staring at me, she put down the joint.

She turned and looked back over her shoulder and waited.

"Show me your ass," I said. I sincerely loved this part.

Eyes locked on mine, she put her thumbs into the waistband of her skirt and panties and slowly pushed them down.

Her ass was architectural triumph of divine origin. And for the moment it was mine.

We sat on a long bench in the soft half darkness of the bedroom, looking into the back garden. The crickets worked away at their nightly labors.

She was wearing the white button-down shirt I'd taken off. Sleeves rolled up, it was as big as a dress. She looked good in anything. She exhaled her Virginia Slim. It was a nice moment. "I love Laurel Canyon."

As did I. After living here and there around the city and then on Arden in Hancock Park for ten years, I'd been back in the canyon for about three. Every now and then, at night, the distant thrum of a car or the scent of the wind through the trees would sync up with an old memory and create a fleeting pocket of three-dimensional wistfulness, bittersweet on the tongue.

Those simple, simplistic, innocent times. And the dreams born of them, now splintered, gray, and ridiculous.

Lynette stubbed out her cigarette. "You ever kill anyone, Dick?"

"That's none of your business."

"That's not an answer."

"That's all you're going to get."

"Come on. You're a full-grown man. Stop being cagey. Tell me, yes or no."

"I'm starting to get black widow vibrations."

"I make you nervous?"

"Not yet."

She picked up a gold ring from a knickknack ashtray on the bookcase. "This always been here?"

"Long as you've been around."

"What is it?" She slid it over her finger, where it rambled around.

I reached over and straightened it up. Like a school ring, it had a large, faceted red stone in an oval setting. "That's an Inter-Services Championship ring."

If you looked closely enough you could see two tiny boxing gloves.

She studied it, me. "You?"

"1988."

I'd caught Marine Lance Corporal Charlton Parker with a perfect left hook eighteen seconds into the first round. Which was lucky because he was scheduled to kill me. I'd fought a series of stiffs and lumps, but Parker was in another league altogether. But the fates weren't with him. The referee raised my hand, and I retired on top.

Lynette studied the ring again. "Badminton?"

"Tiddlywinks."

"You're tough."

"Tough enough."

"I want it."

"You can't have it."

"You'll give me whatever I ask for."

"What do you want?"

"I want to know if you've ever killed anyone." She put the ring down.

"Yes. But that's kill, not execute."

Though the Police Commission had not found the distinction significant. Ending my police career and consigning my friend and partner, Lew Peedner, to the working ranks forever. My former friend and partner.

"You believe in heaven and hell, Dick?"

"I believe that people are more than animals."

"Why?"

"Because I want to believe it."

"But you admit there's no proof."

"Any game is more fun at its highest level of significance." I looked at the point of her nipple through my shirt. "You want me to kill someone for you?"

In a foul old house near Western and Venice I'd caught Elton Reese rising, bloody, from the body of eight-year-old Soon Cha Kim. Reese had raised his hands. "I guess you got me, lawman. I surrender."

That's when I put four bullets into his head.

"Killing someone who deserves to die isn't murder," said Lynette.

"You're right. Sometimes it's manslaughter." I shook my head. "Don't kill anybody. It's too final."

She shrugged, picked up the ring again. "I love my ring, Dick." She laughed. Then she pushed me over and we resumed.

15

CHAPTER FOUR

Near Sundown

I hadn't lasted long as a cop. I wasn't cut out for it. One day, at the station, some genius was praising Nixon. I mentioned a Vietnamese proverb I'd come across. *When a small man casts a long shadow, it's near sundown.*

Deighan scratched his fat ass and uttered the words in which I foresaw the end of my police career. *When a civil servant casts no shadow, it's lunchtime,* he said. Deighan.

There was a big laugh. I shrugged, beat. I was too deep for the room. The next day I ventilated Elton Reese.

CHAPTER FIVE

Chuckie Gregory
and A-1 Contractors

I rolled over Mulholland and let Laurel Canyon Boulevard take me into the valley.

Though many parts of the valley were lush and green, I could never unsee the parched yellowness beneath it all. Buildings budded quickly from the jealous soil, flowered, faded, were razed back into nothingness. Even the newest of the new, like the Laurel Gardenaire, now passing on my left, filled me with fatigue and hopelessness. In ten years it would be run into the ground, full of bug-eyed meth freaks.

I had to get myself out of this mood. It could kill a nice day in the valley.

I'd come over the hill from Hollywood after visiting Mrs. Wagner, my first landlord after I'd gotten out of the service. She'd been seventy-eight then; this very morning, twenty-odd years later, she was ancient, frail as a twig, and barely there.

She lived in a tiny bungalow, now worth a fortune, on Vista below Santa Monica Boulevard. I'd lived over her garage. She served me coffee in the kitchen and showed off the same spoon collection I'd come to know all those years ago. I stirred the weak coffee with a spoon from Vienna, inquired about the problem.

She hunched her fleshless shoulders and pointed her Heidelberg spoon toward the ceiling.

I looked up and understood.

"I had the ceiling replastered, and then it started falling out."

It certainly had. Some know-nothing had fixed up a bad batch of plaster, which dried, separated into pieces the size of an Oreo, and finally succumbed to the forces of Newton.

"A piece fell right into my goldfish bowl."

Now I remembered. She'd always had a fishbowl on the kitchen table. The fish would swim through the little house.

"Finny was killed when plaster fell in." Her thin fingers fluttered around her mouth, and she smiled to let me know she knew she was an old bother. "Finny was my goldfish."

"How much you pay the guy?"

"One thousand five hundred dollars." She paused, embarrassed. "Which is a lot. For me."

"It's a lot for me, too. Let me see what I can do."

"Thank you, Dick," said Mrs. Wagner, touching my hands. With the weight of a butterfly.

"Thank *you*, Mrs. Wagner." I realized I'd never known her first name. But there it was on the contractor's receipt. Delores.

So, on Delores's behalf, I now plied the northernmost stretches of Sepulveda Boulevard, the longest thoroughfare in Los Angeles County. Forty-three miles long. From the South Bay to the mountains.

Finally, off to my right, I saw my destination, the Stanhope Business Park. Single-storied, flat-roofed, baked to a sullen, ocher ugliness, the four long buildings radiating an angry, pitiless heat. The complex begged for a bomb. Or a maniac with a steamroller. Over on the end of Building B was A-1 Contractors, Inc.

I parked the Caddy in a cloud of dust, let it settle, got out, went in.

A-1 Contractors occupied a shallow rectangle. A lazy ceiling fan churned the heat and a cadre of tired flies. A long counter ran most of the way across the room and behind it sat a woman approaching her sixth decade. She put a cigarette into her ashtray.

"May I help you?"

"I'm Dick Henry." I looked at the card Mrs. Wagner had pressed into my hand. "I'm here to see Chuck Gregory."

The woman took a quick drag on her Benson & Hedges. "And the nature of this visit?"

"I'm here on behalf of Mrs. Wagner, eleven thirty-three North Vista Street, in Hollywood. She's having a problem with some work you guys did."

The woman's eyes darted sideways to a closed door. You could hear music. "I'm sorry to hear that, I'm sure we'll make it right."

She reached into a wire basket, took a form off the top, slid it over. "If you could just fill in the particulars." She handed me a stubby yellow pencil.

I never liked forms.

"What about Chuck Gregory? Where's he?"

"Mr. Gregory is on site at the moment. I'm sorry."

"He's not here?"

"No, he's not. If you could fill in the form . . ."

At that moment the music door opened and a big, crew-cut, muscle-bound man stepped out. Thirtyish. Sleeves rolled up, he carried his arms high and wide. "Lydia, I thought I asked you to call—"

Then he saw me. "Uh, yes?"

"Hi," I said, with a pleasant smile. It's always best to start out pleasant. "Mr. Gregory, I presume?"

"Uhhh—"

Of course he was Mr. Gregory. "Mr. Gregory, I'm Dick Henry, and I'm here to talk about the Wagner problem." I smiled. "Should we talk privately?"

I walked into the music room, sat down. Still in the outer office, Crewcut started bitching the woman out.

"Goddammit, Lydia. I told you I wasn't in."

"Then you demonstrated to the contrary."

"Shit. Call Andy and tell him to wait a few. No, just tell him to meet me at Foxy's. Now who's this asshole again?"

"Dick Henry."

"And why's he here?"

"Mrs. Wagner. In Hollywood. You may have replastered her ceiling."

Gregory checked his watch. *May have. May have replastered her ceiling.* Was that a dig? He should fire the old bitch for fucking insolence but good employees were hard to find at the end of the valley and she could juggle huge columns of figures in her head even when she was drunk. Shit. He was going to miss Stormy's turn on the pole. Maybe he'd go for a lap dance. But first maybe he'd have to kick Dick Harvey's ass.

The office was dirty and airless, partially illuminated by a small, smeared window. Not that there was anything to look at. I thought about Mrs. Wagner and felt a spike of active dislike for Chuck Gregory. Guys like this would run over the Mrs. Wagners of the world until they were made to stop.

Gregory entered. "People don't usually just barge into my office." He sat down with a grunt.

I maintained the pleasant tack into the stiffening wind. "Didn't mean to barge, Chuck. Mrs. Wagner must have called six times over the last two weeks."

Crewcut leaned forward over his desk, knit his fingers, rubbed his thumbs together. "Well, we're real busy. Now refresh me on the problem."

"Mrs. Wagner, eleven thirty-three North Vista Street. You, somebody, replastered her ceiling. And it's not working out."

Crewcut decided to turn up the gas. He leaned forward, aggressive. "You a lawyer?"

Somewhere in his recent past was an onion.

I took a small bag of Mrs. Wagner's little plaster cookies, slid it across the desk. "I'm not a lawyer. But this is what I'm talking about. You don't need to be a lawyer."

Chuck fingered the bag, then stared at me. I guess I was supposed to be frightened.

"Am I going to have trouble with you, Harvey?"

Beneath the plane of his desk, my left fist had started to tingle. "The name is Henry. And I sincerely hope there's not going to be trouble."

Chuck got up, started around his desk.

I rose as well. "I just want to make things right."

"Good. That's what small claims court is all about." He was right in my face.

"Actually, that's not good. Mrs. Wagner is three hundred years old. She won't be around for the court's decision." I was giving him a last chance, but I could tell he was too stupid to appreciate my consideration.

An evil smirk stretched Gregory's Teutonic features. "Do I look like the Sympathy Department?"

My left hand had reached full vibratory status. "Not yet," I replied. Then the celestial forces of karma drew my fists forward in a left, right, left to the gut followed by a right upper-cut to the chin, which snapped his teeth together like a dollar mousetrap.

He sailed back into the wall and slid down to a sitting position with a thud.

"Get up, motherfucker." I grabbed his collar and jerked him to his feet, pushed him back into his chair.

Under his chair was his contingency plan, an aluminum baseball bat. He rose and swung. I saw it coming, heard it whistle past my chin, saw it smash the front of his glass souvenir cabinet.

He looked at me, had the sense not to beg; I broke his nose with a straight right.

You know why, in the movies, the sound of breaking bones is simulated by breaking fresh celery? Because breaking bones sounds *exactly* like breaking fresh celery. The battle of A-1 Contractors was over.

"Take out your cashbox, fuckstick, and be quick about it."

He did so.

"Open it, and count out sixteen hundred for Mrs. Wagner."

He did so.

"Now another hundred for Finny."

His eyes questioned who Finny might be, but another honeybee was placed on his desk.

"Now, five hundred for me."

He counted five for me, then sagged back.

I stepped forward and he flinched. "Now listen, Chuckie, to what I'm going to tell you."

Gregory nodded. His shirtfront was a cheerful, sopping crimson.

"It's wrong to take advantage of little old ladies. You get me?"

He got me.

"If you ever do this again, to someone *I know*, I'm going to come back and fuck you up big time. Get me?"

He got me.

"Fly right, Chuckie."

I left his office, shut the door behind me. The lady looked at me. "You punch his lights out, Mr. Harvey?"

I smiled. "Yes, I did."

She lit up a cigarette, exhaled calmly toward the ceiling. "Have a nice day."

I drifted back down Sepulveda. Sometimes the valley was a nice place. Harvey, Henry, what's the diff?

I slid in a Pearly King CD.

Are your blue eyes blue or are they green?
You're the finest thing I've ever seen
I know you're speaking words
I don't know what they mean
Are your blues eyes blue or are they green?
I didn't know till I knew
Baby been waitin' for you
Are your blue eyes blue or are they green?

CHAPTER SIX

No One Files
on Dick Henry

Meanwhile, at the corner of Hollywood and Cahuenga, in a fourth-floor office at the Hollywood Professional Building, Tisdale, gingerly fingering his nose, was in consultation with Myron Ealing, Esquire.

Ealing, who weighed 420 pounds, had his fist elbow deep in a five-gallon tin of stale Christmas popcorn. He was shaking his head from side to side.

On the recommendation of Bobby the Weasel, Tisdale had climbed four flights of stairs to find this monstrous Jabba. And had paid Jabba fifty dollars up-front. But the guy just kept shaking his head.

"What I'm trying to get across, Mr. Tisdale," said Ealing, expectorating a husk of the caramel corn from the tip of his tongue, "is that no one files on Dick Henry."

"What does that mean?" He'd paid fifty for this? "There was a crime committed. My shit is half gone."

"No one files on Dick Henry," repeated Ealing, "nothing comes of it." Good old Dick. Dick knew every clerk in city government. For a crisp, new honeybee and a smile, papers were mutilated, shredded, burned, lost, or damaged by insects.

He just knew too many people. DWP. Edison. The Gas Company. Your death arrow could come from anywhere. That humongous water bill had to be a mistake, but, Christ, clutched in the teeth of the bureaucracy, the details could take weeks to straighten out. In the meantime you went thirsty and couldn't flush your toilet.

Alan Trudeau, that idiot producer, had filed on Dick. Oooo, foolish, so foolish. But Trudeau *was* a fool, the kind who fully believed in the importance of his own importance. In addition to his incredible water bill, $36,000, his new 700 series BMW had been impounded from the safety of his locked garage in his gated community. Paperwork suggested he'd ignored a ticket for an equipment violation. Trudeau did not remember the citation. A king's ransom was demanded for the vehicle's return.

Trudeau had persisted in folly. Subsequently, he found the towing company's byzantine chain of ownership, like a slumlord's, defied legal ascertainment. But charged on a fifteen-minute basis.

An unconnected man had no choice but to capitulate. Trudeau settled for a queen's ransom. With a five-hundred-dollar inconvenience fee. Then his filing was dismissed. Boll weevils had rendered the forms illegible.

"You mean you won't do squat for me," said Tisdale. "Is that what you mean?" At every instance in his whole goddam life, his encounters with the system had been fruitless and negative. Fuck this fat jerk-off.

Ealing eyed the imbecile across his desk. How could he put

it so this fifteen-watt bulb might fully understand a forty-watt concept? "It's like this," said Ealing. "There're only so many ways to fuck a chicken. And you lack the necessities and the technique. And you *don't want* the trouble you're going to get, believe me. My best advice to you is go on home. Or wherever you're living."

"I want my money back."

Myron Ealing rose and pointed to the office door. "Get out of my office."

"Gimme my money."

Graceful as a ballerina, Ealing was around the desk in an instant, looming like a dark cloud. He pointed a cucumber-size finger down at Tisdale. "You paid for my advice. You got it. Do I have to sit on your head?"

Fifty dollars lighter, goddammit, Tisdale set foot on Hollywood Boulevard. Screwed again.

CHAPTER SEVEN

The Green Hat

Myron Ealing had called with a referral. Had Dick heard of Artie Benjamin? Producer?

Producer of what?

In this case, erotica.

Whaddaya mean, in this case?

Shit, Dick, I mean he does porno. Has a little warehouse over there in Van Nuys. Fifty titles. *Buffalo Bill in Hollywood.*

Should I remember that?

Everybody else does.

And the nature of his problem?

His wife.

I arrived at Rexford Drive in Beverly Hills as the sun set. Artie Benjamin's house was a chesty new construction, too big for the lot: plinths, columns, moldings, crowns, fatted grandeur in pastel pink. But all plaster and hollow. You could knock it over with a Subaru.

A Filipino man in black opened the door. His eyes were unblinking mahogany malevolence.

"I'm here to see Mr. Benjamin," I said, pleasantly.

The door was drawn back. The large entryway had been decorated from a catalog and was characterless in a beige, three-star-hotel kind of way.

I was led upstairs into an office.

A banker's lamp filtered green light across a huge desk. Behind the desk a round-shouldered individual, wreathed in smoke, sat back in a tall reclining chair. The Filipino went behind the desk and stood to the man's left side.

My eyes got accustomed to the light. Artie Benjamin was not a handsome man. I put him in his mid-fifties. His face was fleshy and rough, his eyes close set. Dark hair had been artfully arranged on his scalp to make the most out of little. A sharply sculpted mustache drew a fine line between nose and thin lips.

"So you're Dick Henry." He gestured me into the chair across his desk.

"And you're Art Benjamin."

I'd learned a few things about him before my visit. He'd inherited a lot of money from his father who was the national king of cardboard. A regnancy of which I had been previously unaware. The monarch's shadow had been hard to outrun and Artie had never managed. So he did a bit of this, a bit of that, had married and divorced a couple of times here and there.

Then, in Las Vegas, he had crossed paths with an adult film expo and one thing led to another. *Buffalo Bill in Hollywood* had nothing to do with riding horses. But it made $16 million for an investment of $46,000, and suddenly Artie had a career. Some fool had called it art, and Artie had the smarts to shut up. That the spectacular talents of Buffalo Bill's lady saloonkeeper, Thirsty Thelma, were cut short by the self-administration of heroin only added to the dark-star aura of Benjamin's success.

Finally Artie spoke. "Ever been married?"

"Yes."

"Divorced?"

"Yes."

"Ever wear the green hat?"

The green hat. "What does that mean?"

I felt the Filipino's eyes upon me. Impersonal, cold. Like refrigerator beams.

"Your wife. She ever fool around? Was she unfaithful?"

"I don't know. I don't think so."

"You're a man who'd prefer not to know?"

"Knowledge is a dangerous thing."

"Why were you divorced?"

I shrugged. "Generally, strangled communications. Specifically, the unscheduled delivery of a pumpkin pie."

Benjamin wrinkled his nose. "I hate pumpkin pie."

"So do I. What's on your mind, Mr. Benjamin?"

"It's my wife. I want you to find out about her."

"You love her?"

"No." He hadn't liked the question. "But she's mine."

"How old is she?"

"Twenty-nine. I think."

"You got a prenup, right? Why not just divorce her and get it over with?"

"It's not that easy."

"What do you want?"

"I just want to know. One way or the other. Is she cheating. I don't want pictures and all that. I just need to know." Thumb and forefinger ran over his mustache.

"Don't you already know she's cheating?" Of course he did.

"I want to find out for sure."

It was times like these I questioned my vocation as a shortcut man. Every cheating spouse, though all unique human beings and no doubt possessed of wonderful qualities, sang a variation on the same theme. *She/he doesn't understand/know who I really am.*

At that exact moment I felt I'd spent too long exploring the lower aspects of the human condition. I recalled the plumber's piquant umber motto: *your shit is my bread and butter.* Why couldn't I have been satisfied getting my butter as an air-conditioning mechanic?

"I'm told you're the best in the business," said Benjamin.

I decided I didn't want Benjamin's business. "I'm pretty expensive, Mr. Benjamin. Actually, very expensive."

"What's your price?"

"Eight down, seven on delivery of oral report."

"Fifteen large."

"That's right."

"You don't even put it on paper?"

"Nope."

"You are expensive."

Expensive indeed. Maybe I'd head over to Las Brisas and get a few beers with Rojas and company.

"All right." Benjamin pursed his lips and nodded. "Let's do it."

So there it was. Greatness thrust upon me. "All right. Get me some pictures and some numbers and I'll start in." Arnold Kugler, my CPA, would have been proud of me. Honest work.

Benjamin shook his head. "Forget the *Mission Impossible* routine. I'm giving a little shindig Friday night. Why don't you come by and meet the woman herself? I'll introduce you as one of my new associate producers."

Wasn't this lovely.

CHAPTER EIGHT

All the Things You Are

Lynette was sleeping in my bed. I stared down at her. Is a lie a lie when it's told to a beautiful woman? No. Because beautiful women were lies in and of themselves. Without a single word they made extravagant promises. And in the next breath they broke them. Like Lynette. Like Julia.

Though Julia wasn't half as lovely as Lynette. But she did have a certain, undeniable architectural appeal.

I'd met Julia during my Navy days in Pearl. In those days, convinced my personality congealed in the presence of beauty, I had taken Julia to a jazz club. Where if conversation ran dry I'd be able to snap my fingers and pretend no words were necessary.

Up front, a balding, thirty-year-old man with a wandering eye, Martin Levy, presided over a battered white Steinway like a praying mantis.

After a couple of tunes, Julia turned to me and asked a question I might have paid her to ask. She motioned toward Levy. "How do you know if a guy can really play or if he's just fooling around?"

I played a little guitar back then, in Clapton's name, and had recently perused several articles on jazz improvisation.

According to somebody, "All the Things You Are" stood far above all other songs, improvisation-wise. If you could blow over the chord changes in that song, written by Jerome Kern, whoever he was, you could call yourself a righteous jazz musician. I imparted this lore to Julia and watched her breasts heave in gratitude.

"You know an awful lot about jazz, Dick. I'm really impressed."

Impressed? With that my tongue was loosed and I commenced foreplay. I dropped a few paragraphs about vertical and horizontal improvisation. The difference between the styles of bebop Charlie Parker and cool Miles Davis.

On the small bandstand, a perspiring Martin Levy finished up his set to decent applause. Then he stood around, mopping his forehead, waiting to be appreciated.

I walked up front with a pleased Julia. As I wondered which eye was looking at me, I tailored a careful compliment, specific enough so he'd realize I knew something about music. But Julia beat me to it.

"I like your horizontal improvisations," she prattled.

"Really? Far out." Levy was apparently delighted. "What about my verticals?"

"Those, too," said Julia solemnly.

Levy grinned and I knew, in his head, he was tickling her tonsils.

He returned to the both of us. "People like you guys are so cool," he gushed. "That's who I'm playing for. That's *why* I play." An eye rolled over Julia's big breasts.

Well, fuck the both of you, I thought. We'll see how good you really are, you one-eyed eater-of-dung. I shot a chilled glance toward Julia, then turned to Cyclops. "Can you play a tune for us?"

He waggled fat, stubby fingers, smiled. "For you guys, anything. What do you want to hear?"

"Could you play 'All the Things You Are'?" By that guy. The suggestion stopped Piano Man in his tracks.

I eyed Julia. *See.*

" 'All the Things You Are'?" Levy looked a little flinty.

Poseur pays the price. And keep your fucking eye off Julia's tits. "I dunno." I shrugged carelessly. "Maybe it's not your bag."

"Actually, man," said Levy, "it is my bag. I just played it."

If I'd had the resources, I would've asked him to play it again and play it right this time. But I had no such resources. I was rooted to the spot and vacant of all intelligence.

Julia turned, looked at me as if I had six legs and had crawled out from under the nightstand. Her nose was a little long, I realized. And one ear sat a little higher than the other.

In any case, that was how Julia met Martin Levy and started her long descent into addiction, HIV, and death.

And that same incident was one of the signposts helping me conclude music was not my life path.

I was destined to become the Shortcut Man.

Lynette stirred, opened one eye, smiled at me, pulled me into bed. Touching is not a lie.

CHAPTER NINE

You Know My Wife?

The Caddy purred west on Sunset. The neon always cheered me up. Fuck Julia.

I checked my watch. I would be fashionably late to Artie Benjamin's porno soiree.

The street was parked up. A college kid from the valet service in a USC jacket was making tickets and directing things. After two Lexi, I was next.

Richie Rich was not impressed with Detroit's finest circa 1969. He leaned in, bored, pointed down the street. "Deliveries in the rear."

I grabbed him by the tie, pulled him close. "Then bend over, darling." After a quiet, intimate moment, we achieved a new level of understanding.

"Maybe, uh, you're going to the party," he reasoned.

"And you want to park my car."

It so happened he did.

The place was packed. I didn't know a soul. I began to wonder what were the duties of an associate producer. Though it seemed anyone could probably do it.

My time in Hollywood had vaguely acquainted me with

the duties of a regular producer. It was a matter of gathering. Gathering money, resources, favors, people. Bringing them all together at the exact moment the whole exceeded the sum of the parts. Holding it all together when the dream deflated into reality. Substituting Toronto for New York, Arcadia for Beverly Hills, Chevrolet for a Cadillac. Every so often it worked out and your name went on the side of a bus that rolled through neighborhoods where no one spoke English.

I ran into seven associate producers before I finished my first drink. I had not as yet seen my host. I hoped he remembered inviting me. I shrugged to myself. He had eight thousand reasons to remember. Or to forget.

Then I spied him and we walked toward the rear of the house.

Not all of the partygoers seemed to know their host. Benjamin gestured at them. "All the friends that money can buy."

Then I saw Benjamin's Filipino with a tray of drinks. "Have you seen Judy?" Benjamin asked him.

The Filipino nodded, his eyes transmitting a careful message not meant for me.

Benjamin was impatient, waved him off. "Never mind all that. Where is she?"

The Filipino indicated toward the rear of the house with his shoulder, sniffed twice, quickly.

"Thank you, Arnuldo," said Benjamin. Then he turned to me. "Judy is snorting coke in the back."

Whatever gets you through the night. Though, on a moral scale, if you sifted long enough, things fell into two categories. Right or wrong. No middle ground. No neutral. "Lead onward," I urged my host.

We passed other behaviors, sexual and chemical, on the way through the house. Inhibitions had been long lost. It would be a five-maid cleanup team on the morrow.

Finally, through the windows of the game room—Ping-Pong, pool, air hockey, backgammon—a knot of figures became visible in silhouette on the porch.

The group was in high hilarity, each bending in turn to a small, shiny plane.

Benjamin's face reflected the fact that they were getting high on his dime. "Judy," he called in a friendly fashion.

I could see just one woman among them. The woman ignored Benjamin, bent down to the mirror once again.

"Judy." This time Benjamin's voice contained a shred of a parent being patient.

"Oh, for chrissakes, Artie," said the woman, not turning around.

Laughter from the knot.

Benjamin smiled at me to reassure me he had not been disrespected. "Judy, there's someone here I want you to meet."

"O-ka-ay, Lieutenant."

More laughter.

I could see the tension in his jaw. He smiled at me again. Plainly artificial. Had he forgotten why I was here? Or was it a husband's natural response to cuckoldry?

The woman took a last toot, spun away from the gang, and walked into the game room.

My Bloody Mary slipped through my fingers and shattered on the floor.

Lynette.

Lynette was Judy.

Judy was Lynette.

"Sorry," I managed, feeling my face go hot.

"Dick, this is my wi——"

But Judy came forward, cut him off, thrust her hand out. "Hi, I'm Judy Benjamin."

We shook.

"Glad you could come. And don't worry about the glassware." In shards at her feet. "It's cheap shit we bought for the party. Artie will buy more."

"I'm Dick Henry." Suddenly I was a bad actor. I glued a smile on my face.

Judy looked around, then back at me. "You've made quite a mess, Dick. I bet you make messes all the time."

She looked at Artie. "Where's Arnuldo?"

Arnuldo appeared with whisk broom and dustpan and got to work.

"Can Arnuldo get you another drink?" Judy was absolutely cool.

"No, thanks."

Arnuldo finished up, eyed me, disappeared.

Benjamin stepped in, clapped me on the shoulder. "I've just hired Dick as an associate producer for one of my projects."

Judy appraised me with new eyes, apparently. "Well, well, well. An associate producer. There's a rare breed. What project are you going to be working on?"

How the hell did I know?

Benjamin stepped in, another bad actor. "He'll be working on *Rubber Babies.*"

"*Rubber Babies.* What's the premise?" She looked right into my eyes.

"Friction." I was recovering somewhat, and shock had turned into anger.

Judy laughed.

Benjamin smiled through his teeth. "That actually wouldn't be a bad title."

"Do I have to join the Writers Guild?" I was getting comfortable on my new horse.

"Can you write?" she asked.

"No."

"Then you've got a future."

Benjamin studied us both. Then he put his hand on my arm, addressed his wife. "Excuse us, my darling. There're a few other people I think Dick should meet."

Judy nodded. "Nice meeting you, Mr.————." My last name had slipped her mind.

"Henry," I filled in. "Dick Henry. Nice meeting you, too."

She smiled and returned to the porch.

Benjamin and I walked back the way we'd come, but he seemed preoccupied and didn't introduce me to anyone. *Of course.* I'd half forgotten I was playing a role. He headed up to his office, gestured me to follow.

Shutting the door, he took a seat behind his desk, opened up the desk drawer, pulled out a mirror and a small vial. He emptied the vial on the mirror, started chopping up the coke with an Armani charge card. "You do this shit?"

I shook my head. "No thanks. I got other ways to blow my money." Like alimony and child support. "But don't mind me."

He didn't. He chopped some more, then dug in his drawer again, retrieved a silver straw. The prehit ritual was complete. Then and only then. He huffed a huge line. He blinked, leaned back, sighed. "All I need now . . . is one more."

A man takes the shit. The shit takes the shit. The shit takes the man.

Again he poured, chopped, and railed. Then disposed of his handiwork, looked up. "Well, that was my wife."

"That was your wife."

Then he leaned back and regarded me. "I got one question for you, Mr. Henry." He tipped his head to one side, as if to truly observe me. "You, uh, *know* my wife?"

I looked him right in the eye. "Sure I do, Mr. Benjamin. But I didn't know she was married. To you. To anyone. I've been whacking her with the Dick-stick for three, four months."

How about that for the cold, naked truth?

Benjamin opened his drawer, took out a huge handgun. He aimed it at my face and pulled the trigger.

That's how they found me. With my head blown off.

I drove the Caddy eastward on Sunset. I could see the western-most lights of the strip. The wind was cool and refreshing.

Of course I didn't say that.

I had a chance to say something, but, in an instant, the time to speak up was irrevocably behind me and I was launched down the river of prevarication, committed to an unknown series of actions.

And what about Lynette?

Fuck Lynette.

CHAPTER TEN

And I Fell

There was a knock at my door later that night. I knew it was her. I considered not opening it but I wanted to kill her so I did.

"Fuck. You." My first words.

"Dick."

"Fuck you."

"Are you going to invite me in or just curse me on your doorstep?"

"Fuck it. Come in, Mrs. Benjamin."

In she came.

"I don't know what to say to you, I really don't." Except I knew all along something like this was coming, just didn't know the moment of its arrival. My heart was smashed into a million pieces anyway. Of course, she had made herself up from nothing. How could I not know? How could Benjamin not know?

"You could just say hello, Dick."

"Fuck you. *Judy.*"

"I'm sorry, Dick."

"You're *sorry*. About what, may I ask? That your husband has hired me to find out who you're fucking?"

A silence.

"And how in Christ's name did he call *me* anyway?"

"I don't know, Dick."

"What a fucking mess."

"I'm sorry I hurt your feelings."

"Yeah, I guess you did. Because the person you met—the person you met was me—pretty close to me, anyway." Like I said. No man is entirely honest with a beautiful woman. He knows better.

"Dick—"

"And why the name *Lynette,* for chrissakes? Where did that come from?"

"It was my secret name for myself. The person I wanted to be instead of the person I was. The person I tried to give to you. And I gave you all the me I could give you."

Her words and the sound of her words disgusted me. Each a splintered mirror of my stupidity.

"You"—I pointed at her—"are a cold-assed *liar.* And now, you and I, *you and I God help us,* we're in real trouble."

"No, we're not."

"Yes, we are. He may be an asshole but he's got brains. Has it occurred to you that his hiring me might not be a coincidence? He straight-out asked me if I knew you."

"What did you say?"

"I fucking lied. What do you think?"

Quieter now. "Artie won't hurt anyone."

I rubbed thumb and forefinger. "Money! Money! He has the *means* to hurt people. And look at what's-his-name. Arnuldo. That's what he does. He hurts people. And if something tears Artie's blinders off and he realizes that he's just a chump with a whore for a wife and nothing to lose—then he's dangerous. Really dangerous."

"I guess you keep him in the dark."

"What else?" I needed the dark myself.

I walked back to the bedroom where the window looked out into the cool. Only the crickets were busy. I envied their purpose of mind.

The floor creaked. She'd followed me in. I should've turned around, kicked her in the ass, and told her to get the hell out.

I felt her hand upon my shoulder. Smelled the trace of perfume that floated off her wrist.

"Make love to me."

I didn't move. "Get outa here. Just go."

"Dick."

"We're not capable of making love, you and me. *I don't even know your name.* We're just capable of fucking." I stared out into the garden darkness.

Her voice was a wet whisper. "So, fuck me, Dick."

I spun around to slap her. She didn't flinch. She put her face up.

"Go ahead, hit me. I deserve it."

I just stood there, then grabbed her hair and threw her onto the bed. She laughed. Crookedly.

I didn't bother with her blouse, just took her pants, ripped them down. She kicked out of them with a moan. At the jade gate I pulled her panties to the side. I brought my finger up from below, and it slipped right in. She didn't need any warm-up. I tore the panties down but not off, rolled her knees up, slapped her ass hard, back and forth, *whack whack,* pushed her legs back and went in.

We rode like the devil was behind us. I was filled with rage and a ferocious body joy at the same time and knew I was in total control. I took her through the clouds and rain over and over and over and finally sighted it for myself. I went up the

mountain like a soldier beyond concern of life or death and at
the top of all things she drew her nails down my back and I
exploded into nothingness, separated all the cells of my being,
then fell back into myself, through myself, a neutron star of
ultimate and painful density, then I was on the other side and a
second wave approached and I thought it was impossible but I
went up and over, helpless, disintegrated again, low and beautiful, grinding, utter agony, strung atom by atom, then I fell
and I fell and I fell and I fell.

PART TWO

Coils of
the Beast

CHAPTER ELEVEN

Water Hammer

In the middle of the night I woke up, made myself a glass of ice water, walked back to the bedroom. She was sleeping.

If you believed in God, it was not hard to imagine His love for her. The subtle arches of her eyebrows, the delicate curves of her ears, the ruddy fullness of her lips, her porcelain skin, the miraculous, mysterious line of demarcation where her black black hair began on that unlined forehead. I could look, look again, and look again.

I believe that deep in a man's soul, never glimpsed by his conscious mind, is his personal template of ideal beauty. And the closer the contemplated is to this unknown ideal, the more qualities we are willing to lend, and the easier it is to fall in love with them.

Lynette was plainly amoral, possibly evil. But, looking into her face, I could see only compassion, kindness, and goodness. So here I sat, between Benjamin and Lynette, my loyalties divided and paralyzed, realizing the impossibility of serving two masters.

What did she want? Lynette had told me her story, but since her name was not even Lynette, who knew what was bullshit.

High school diploma in hand, she'd run away from home,

Mt. Clemens, near Detroit. Armed only with Joyce's *Ulysses,* of which she claimed no man had read past the first three chapters, she survived a bus trip to San Bernardino. But somehow, sleep-deprived, she hadn't disembarked and ended up in Long Beach.

She'd gotten a job at a coffee shop, met a kid named Brett Russell. From Wisconsin. He was in the Navy. They'd gotten engaged. He was the love of her life. His ship, the *St. Louis,* an amphibious cargo something or other, departed on West-Pac. Between Long Beach and Pearl, Russell had fallen, had jumped, or had been pushed over the side. Conclusions aside, he wasn't onboard when they reached the islands.

But no one informed her of anything, engagement was an unofficial condition. She just never heard from him again. She thought she'd been abandoned. At the free clinic, Dr. Lim told her she was pregnant. Her stepmother told her not to come home. She had an abortion ten days later. There were complications. She could no longer conceive. Which was okay with her. She never wanted brats.

Nine months later the *St. Louis* returned to Long Beach. A shipmate of Brett's, Joey Long, ran into her and told her the bad news. She and Joey got close. Close enough. It was a rebound thing.

They got married in a funky wedding chapel on Pine Avenue and moved into the little apartment she and Brett used to share. The plumbing in the place was weird. Sounded like someone was banging on the pipes.

"Water hammer," I'd said.

Lynette had laughed. "That was it! That's what Joey called it."

"Joey was a machinist's mate. Or a boiler tech."

"A machinist's mate! With the little propeller on his shoulder." She'd shaken her head. "I can hardly remember his face.

I'd cook these wretched little dinners and we'd watch TV, smoke pot, and screw. We'd go to the Navy Exchange and buy cheap cigarettes. We had a stereo with a thousand buttons and switches but it only worked on AM. On one speaker."

She'd lit up a cigarette. "One day we'd run out of pot and the place was a wreck. Joey went out with his friends. And I caught myself thinking, Who *is* this guy? It was basically over."

"There wasn't a grand finale?"

"Oh, there was a finale. He got caught sniffing butyl nitrate or something on a duty night. And fucking the radioman."

"I didn't think they had women on those ships."

"They didn't."

"They didn't what?"

"Have women on the ship."

"Oh. *Oh.*" It takes me a while.

"Which was the real problem."

"Joey liked dudes."

"Joey walked both sides of the street." She laughed. "So we got a divorce and I drifted up to Vegas."

Beauty stretched, an angel gently recalled to life. Her eyes alighted upon me, and the corners of her mouth turned up. "Make love to me, Dick," she said.

I looked at her, and all dark things washed out of my mind.

CHAPTER TWELVE

The Tale
of Johnny Santo

The next morning she was gone. Good. I had work to do and needed to think. Or not to think. I made a thick cup of black coffee, and Rojas knocked at the door.

It was impossible to be depressed in Rojas's company. He just wouldn't let you. He sauntered into the kitchen, tossed his jacket over a chair, sat down. He took one look at my face, shook his head. "Fuck you," he said.

Immediately I felt better.

He sparked a joint, took a deep draft. "So *whazzup*, white man?"

"Nothing."

"Looks like something happened last night."

"Well, it didn't."

"Whatever you say, dude." He snorted. "You know you can't hold nothin' back from me."

An old friend, Jonathan, had once called me fibissedah-face. Yiddish. Meaning all my feelings paraded across my mug, clearly to be read. I remembered his comment and adopted a purposeful neutrality.

"You ain't foolin' nobody," said Rojas.

I told him about a roach coach, a bad burrito, and immigrant bathtub cheese.

"Horseshit," said Rojas.

I offered breakfast and he accepted. I made my special scrambled eggs with sourdough toast. As he ate, I explained how, during a fragrant portion of my marriage, I had been called the Egg King.

"Bullshit," said Rojas.

Well, all right. Actually, I called myself the Egg King.

I explained the morning's mission. Five minutes later we were cruising down Sunset to the beach. It was a nice, sunny ride, not too hot. We made a right at Gladstone's and rolled north on PCH to Topanga.

Topanga Canyon was the last Los Angeles habitat of that disappearing species, the hippie. Pushed out of Laurel Canyon by rising rents, they were faced with two choices, becoming the man or fleeing the man to Topanga.

Eventually they'd be pushed out of Topanga, too. But not quite yet. We passed the Fernwood Market and then some, made a left at Old Topanga.

It was rural, peaceful, and every Angeleno driving these roads considered chucking everything and living here. Where the air was invisible. But the reality was, unless you could conjure enough money to facilitate your lifestyle, opulent or meager, it was just too far from the ant farm.

On top of a gentle hill we saw an address on a mailbox, pulled in, drove down a long driveway.

"Who are these people again?"

"The Hartfords."

"Right. And who's the dude?"

"Sky Blue." Chances were good Sky Blue was a hippie.

We knocked on the door, heard footsteps, then met the Hartfords.

He was tall and skinny but crooked, his wife was not quite five feet. She tipped her head, squinted belligerently at me. It looked like she wore the pants. Certainly a more perfect union.

"Are you him?" she asked.

"I'm Dick Henry; this is my associate, Enrique Montalvo Rojas."

"You're the short shrift man?"

"Maybe." I had no idea how long my shrift was, or if indeed I possessed one, or any. "What *is* a shrift?"

"It means penance," said her husband. "Short shrift was a quick penance a sinner could complete before absolution and execution."

The human condition. You're sentenced to death and still they're rushing you.

The woman suddenly concluded we were the right guys, invited us in, introduced herself. "I'm Sara. This is my husband—"

"Roland."

We passed through the living room done western style and out onto a back veranda.

"This is the problem," said Sara.

All it took was a glance. I'd been told, by the Hartfords' son, who was paying me, that a man in a tent wouldn't leave. Which sounded easy enough.

But what I was confronting was a settlement. There was the Army tent. But above it was a huge orange silk parachute wired to a spreading oak tree. Under the parachute's generous circumference I saw a lean-to, a fire pit, some water jugs, a stack of rabbit cages, two chicken coops, a recliner upholstered in ragged leatherine, five or six junk bicycles, two shopping carts, three or four differing chairs, a table with three legs and a cinder block, some spindly pole lamps, a collection of toilet bowls, and a garden with some marijuana cultivation.

"I let Sky put in a tent. Temporarily." Sara looked up at me. I nodded. "And one thing led to another." What we had here was a zoning problem.

"Did you ask him to vacate the premises?"

"Yes."

"But?"

"But he said he wasn't ready."

And grew less ready every day.

She pointed to the marijuana. "See. He does like the Indians did."

Rojas looked at me, then at Sara. "Like the Indians did what, ma'am?"

"He smokes his corn all day long," said Sara. "They called it maize."

So there you have it.

The Hartfords retreated. Rojas shook his head, looked at me accusatively. "I ain't no handyman, ese."

I'd been thinking the same thing. Then I had an idea. I tapped at the back door. "Mrs. Hartford, do you have any twine?"

"Twine? Oh, yes we do!" piped up Roland, over her shoulder, with a triumphant look at his wife.

In fact, Roland had one of the world's largest balls of twine still in captivity. Its girth dominated the toolshed. Good, sturdy stuff, Christmas tree quality.

One more question. "Can I drive my Cadillac into the backyard?"

"Sky wouldn't like that," said Sara, clucking. "Is it a green vehicle?"

No, it's not.

"Go right ahead," said Roland.

A green vehicle? That meant Sky wouldn't immediately appreciate the mighty horsepower of a 472-cubic-inch, eight-cylinder engine, the largest production-run power plant in the history of the Motor City.

I explained my plan to Rojas. He laughed. We got our twine and set to.

After a bit he looked over at me. "I didn't tell you, dude. Gloria and I are, uh, we're through."

Gloria was Rojas's wife. I liked Gloria. And I liked Rojas. And I liked them together. "Through? Why?"

"I dunno. I was lookin' at her the other night, she was making something in the kitchen, and I thought to myself, I don't know this woman. I don't *know* her. She's a stone stranger. It was deep. It was freaky."

"You never know anybody."

"Don't you think you should?"

"I'm not sure. I'm not sure it helps."

"What about you and the stewardess chick? You told me how much you were diggin' on her."

"I said that?"

"You said that."

"I don't know her at all."

"You're fucked up."

I *was* fucked up. I couldn't get the situation out of my mind. The new equilibrium, if there was to be one, was way off. The floor had been pulled from beneath my feet.

An old memory flickered to life, back from Navy days. Once a year or so I'd venture back to L.A. from wherever I was stationed. My good friend Joe, in celebration, always took me up to the Mulholland Club. It was a big, white snobatorium above

Mulholland Drive, looking down on the lights of the valley. Joe would leave his car with the valet crew, we'd enter grandly, flirt with the staff, swim, use the sauna, the weight room, eat in the dining room, have a ball.

In the last year of my enlistment, I asked Joe a question as we changed into our trunks.

"Joe," I said, "we've been coming up here forever. How come you always put your shoes and stuff on *top* of the locker—instead of *in* the locker?"

"Oh, that's simple," said Joe, peeling off a sock. "I'm not a member."

In that instant I made transit from prince to weasel, spent my last hours at the Mulholland Club on tiptoe, grinning at the staff. Joe had a grand old time, as always. Hey, Joe, I miss you.

Rojas straightened up, hands at his back, surveyed our work. "We're done here."

We went back to the house, the Hartfords poured us some lemonade.

"You're going to need a hauler," I said. "You know one?"

"Bill at Fernwood," said Sara.

A shadow crossed the window. "I think that's Sky," said Roland in a small voice.

I stood up. "We'll go have a talk with him."

In the backyard, a huge, bearded, big-bellied, middle-aged man with very long hair and a kerchief had spied the Caddy and was looking around. He very much resembled Blackbeard the pirate. He weighed in at about 350. He turned, thunder on his brow.

"Yo. What the fuck here?"

I turned to Rojas. "I think this is Sky Blue."

"No shit."

"Prepare to drive on my signal."

Rojas appeared disappointed. "How come you always get the fun part?"

"All right." I pulled a quarter out of my pocket, flipped it. "Call it."

"Tails."

Heads.

Rojas walked for the Cadillac.

I felt that twinge of anticipation as Sky Blue closed on me. He had not seen the twine or divined its purpose. "Would you be Mr. Blue?" I inquired affably. Affable is my starting point.

Blackbeard ignored my demonstration of gracious living. "That old piece of shit your car?"

You don't hit someone for bad-mouthing your car. But his rudeness forced me to consider his aura. It was reddish and dark, running to violence. I wondered if the fates would summon me to directly adjust his celestial trajectory. "I'm Dick. I'm here to help."

"Help?"

"Mrs. Hartford says you been smoking too much corn. So you're moving."

Across the yard, Rojas started up the Cadillac.

Sky's eyes narrowed. "I ain't goin' nowhere, dude. Who the fuck says I'm moving?"

"I do." I measured Sky Blue's chin.

"I dare you," said Blackbeard.

"Okay." I signaled to Rojas.

Rojas stepped on the gas, the Caddy moved forward, snapping the slack out of the heavy twine. The first thing that moved was one of the shopping carts. It leapt into the air. A second later, in its entirety, the settlement was ripped from it moorings. The tent, the parachute, the cages, the coops, the bicycles, the chairs, the shopping carts, the pakalolo, the recliner, everything—everything was pulled through high grass and down the driveway.

Fifteen seconds later, the only thing left was a big cloud of dust.

Sky stared, slack-jawed, at the location where so recently the ciudad de ganja had metastasized. He turned to me, eyes bulging with rage. I stepped back, ready to launch the karma missile.

Then Blackbeard burst into tears.

I hit him anyway. A straight overhand right to the chin. Down went Sky Blue.

We rolled him into the backseat, drove him down the canyon, stopped across the street from Fernwood Market.

The sissy was still sobbing. I turned around. "Knock that crying shit off, buddy, or Mr. Rojas will beat the living piss out of you."

"O-okay."

Now that we had him off-property it was time for skillful intimidating threats, ensuring his nonreturn.

"You know who Johnny Santo is?" I began.

"Y-yeah," said Sky.

"You do?" I'd made the name up out of thin air.

"He makes pizza at Andre's."

"Not that Johnny Santo, asshole. The one who's part of the Bonanno family. They own Los Angeles. Sara Hartford is his aunt by marriage. He told us to barbecue your nuts."

"A la carte," detailed Rojas.

"You go back up there, Sky, ever again, Johnny Santo will rip out your tongue and stuff it up your ass with a fork. Now get the fuck out of here."

Sky Blue got out. A breeze came up and blew him toward

Fernwood Market. Like a plastic bag, he would end up some-where he did not belong. But not with the Hartfords and not my problem.

Then, halfway to the market, he turned and came back. "Hey. You guys got a joint?"

Fuck *you*. The nerve.

Rojas and I headed back to Hollywood. I shook my head. "The balls of that asshole."

"Strange balls," said Rojas. Which reminded me of that song by Cream. He lit up his joint, looked at me. "At least we know where Johnny Santo works."

"Andre's."

Rojas snickered. *"Johnny Santo."*

"It sounded good at the time. Like a bad motherfucker."

He took another poke. "Not so bad, I guess." He exhaled in a satisfied manner. "You know"—he paused—"Gloria and I aren't really through."

"You're not?"

"Nah, I don't think so, man."

"You figure you really *do know her*?"

"No. But hell, I don't know nobody. Like you. You could be anyone. Who the fuck are you? I mean who the fuck *are* you?"

Who the fuck *was* I? Lately I'd been a little disappointed. "I don't know who I am. I just show up every day."

"That's fucked up, dude."

"Well, who are you?"

"Enrique Montalvo Rojas."

Like I said. You couldn't be depressed in Rojas's company. He was probably a Mayan prince. I handed him an envelope containing five honeybees.

He put the envelope in his pocket, nodded, smiled. "Thank you, brother."

CHAPTER THIRTEEN

Marriage
and Temptation

I couldn't get Lynette off my mind. I'd been a goddam fool. And would've continued being a fool. And maybe I was a fool all over again. Starting last night.

And fool Benjamin. To whom I'd promised results in two or three weeks. Why in hell had Benjamin married her? He couldn't have believed a girl like Lynette, like Judy, would fall in love with him, could he?

But of course he could. A man's capacity to delude himself is voluminous and rife with opportunity. Equipped with a magic mirror at birth, he works a lifetime to improve its reflectivity. Eventually, when nature demanded, the comb-over and the Orlon toupee would pass muster.

Luckily, I still looked pretty good.

I'd been married before. Marriage is a funny proposition. It requires all one's good qualities and often calls forth one's worst. You wouldn't drive to Fresno in a car that had a fifty percent chance of breaking down over the Grapevine, yet, at the pass line, I mean the altar, millions of gamblers try their luck and bet their lives.

My own marriage I had blown out of the water three years ago. Georgette and I had been married twelve years, and I really couldn't tell how I felt about things any longer. Love, duty, habit, children, fatigue—it was all a mishmash. I began to wonder if I was capable of fucking—versus the more sedate activity of making love. Not that making love was bad once we set a date, cleared the schedule, made dinner for the kids, and got around to harnessing the love machine. Without falling asleep from pure exhaustion.

Temptation presented itself, and I succumbed directly.

Kiera Allen was Arnold Kugler's secretary. Kugler was my CPA years earlier. I'd rescued him from the snares of a blackmailer.

Kiera was a very pretty, dark-headed woman whom I'd flirted with a hundred times. She looked up from her desk with a smile, chewing her gum with tidy, efficient mastications. "Mr. Kugler wanted you to sign both of these. He asked me to apologize for not being here."

She slid the documents across her desk, opened her gold fountain pen, very slowly slid the cap over the barrel, and handed it to me in a significant manner. I caught a glimpse of cleavage and a whiff of perfume.

"Thank you, Kiera."

"You're welcome, Mr. Henry," said Kiera. She had china blue eyes.

I had just come from a disagreeable discussion with Georgette about stuff in the garage. What was the big deal? No one I knew could park more than one car in a two-car garage. Stuff took over. *Stuff* took *space*. Not only that, I had just been paid a good sum for a particularly clever piece of work. I was picked on and unappreciated.

I signed Kugler's documents slowly, largely. I recalled that the size of space-containing letters, *o, d, e, p, b,* et cetera, was a measure of ego. Portly. My ego that day was portly.

Kiera looked up at me. "You have large hands."

"Yes, I do," I replied, realizing I was standing at a precipice. I looked into her eyes.

She stared back.

I went forward. "Can I cut to the chase?"

Kiera looked down before she looked up. "What, uh, do you mean?"

I leaned down, into the fragrant vicinity of her ear, whispered my intentions. Kiera's eyes went wide and she swallowed her gum.

CHAPTER FOURTEEN

Pussy

Not that I loved pussy a la carte. Regardless of what I had suggested to Kiera Allen. But sometimes it was the means to an end.

I recalled my first advice on the matter. It had come from a seventh-grade classmate, Ted, a shameless and notorious liar. Not only had he done everything known to man, he had done it twice or had done it better. You ever steal a car? Stole a Ferrari. From a prince. Ever hook a worm? Wrestled an anaconda. Ever fuck a midget? Sure. Once in Bakersfield, once in Victorville.

He imparted the great pussy-eating secret at recess. *You just get down there and say Mississippi.* Of course, I nodded, everybody knows that. Secretly I was confused. You just got down there and said Mississippi to *what*? And why Mississippi? Why not Monongahela?

I kept my peace on the subject for years. Not that I was adverse to exaggeration or the outright lie on more general subjects, like communism, or ninja technique, but here I felt a natural trepidation about discussing what I might be called upon to specifically describe. The vagina was a mysterious organ, an inverse organ one might say; even its exact location was undefined. Like the Spice Islands. It was *down there.*

My second significant pussy tutorial was in Navy boot camp, San Diego. Our company commander, Kennington, had determined, on the way home from the White Pig, to awaken his recruits for a lecture. He was three sheets to the wind and filled with a poisonous wrath toward all humanity and his company of recruits in particular.

The lights flickered on in the barracks. But not prefaced by reveille. Something was up. Then I heard Kennington.

"Get up, you greasy little lambs," he screamed at the top of his lungs.

Hurriedly we assembled, standing at attention near our bunks, dressed in our skivvies, swaying in early consciousness.

Kennington railed at us for our failings, our putrid hopes and dreams, our feminine characters. Of one phenomenon, however, we should have no fear. Drowning. We should not fear drowning because, sure as God made little green apples, He had decreed that shit would float. We would be safe but soggy.

Then, naturally, the subject turned to pussy. "You shitheads know how to eat pussy?" He sprayed the nearest among us with spittle.

We stood silent.

Which Kennington could not abide. "Did you hear me, *ladies?*" He dripped scorn from every syllable. "I asked you assholes a question. You assholes know how to eat pussy?"

A few of the liars among us ventured that they did. I held my peace. Even though I had plumbed the great mystery, going *down there* and lapping assiduously. Albeit in an indiscriminate manner.

"What you do," continued Kennington in high bellow, "what you do is get down there and find the little man in the boat. That's who you gotta find. The little man in the boat."

He searched the faces of his recruits as if his advice had been self-evident. "Who do you have to find?" he queried savagely.

"The, uh, man in the boat," was the weak, uncertain response.

"Who do you have to find?" Kennington had grown purple-faced in fury. How did it come to be that he, lustrous Kennington, had to instruct these limp-wristed ladies in something he was born knowing? Christ Jesus, he was an expert in utero. "Who do you have to find?"

"The *little* man in the boat," we chorused.

"Who?"

Now we knew our line. "The little man in the boat," we yelled. Our roar of certitude echoed through the barracks, the base, through all of San Diego.

In the silence that followed, Recruit Crudeldorf raised a tentative hand.

"Yes, you maggot?" snarled Kennington.

"Uhh, where *is* the little man in the boat?" asked Crudeldorf, speaking for many.

Shit. That would be Mississippi.

CHAPTER FIFTEEN

Francie Must Die

I awoke the next morning with business on my plate. I headed over to the Farmers Market, Third and Fairfax, grabbed a cup of coffee at Bob's Donuts, sat under a ficus tree, waited for my new client.

Betty Fraiden, fiftyish, had come on behalf of her father, Franklin Tillman. Mr. Tillman had entered into correspondence with a woman in the Philippines. The relationship had turned pecuniary. Mrs. Fraiden showed me a sheaf of letters.

"You think these are for real, Mr. Henry?"

As Ms. Fraiden picked up some gumbo on the back patio, I read the whole batch, accumulated over a year. Like a well-composed piece of music, the letters started simply and waxed to a sublime and noble passion. With a secondary theme of darkness, deprivation, and tragedy. Mr. Tillman had offered financial assistance at the halfway point. Francie, with deep reservations, had accepted.

The English in the letters was bad, purposely bad, I decided, not ignorant or careless. The penmanship, however, was uniform and excellent, with care to detail. It's not that this dichotomy wasn't possible, but it rang an alarm bell.

"Do you have the envelopes these came in?"

There were envelopes but no postmarks, no addresses. Just the name "Mr. Franklin" centered on every envelope in the same careful hand.

"Where do the letters come from?"

"Father is a member of the St. Paul of Tarsus congregation. These come in the biweekly post from a sister congregation in Manila."

"How much has he lost?"

"Fourteen thousand, in around there. Maybe a little more."

"St. Paul. The place at Gardner and Hollywood?"

"You must know the area."

"My first job. A paper route around there."

"Small world."

"As long as you don't have to paint it."

"You think Dad's being ripped off?"

"Probably. How'd you find out?"

"He said he had really good news. I thought it was bingo. Then he said he was going to get married. My teeth nearly fell out."

"How old's your dad?"

"Seventy-eight."

"What does he think?"

"He's in love, for godsake."

Silly old fuck. No fool like an old fool. But who could blame him? When Mr. Tillman looked in the mirror, who deserved to be loved more than Franklin? Behind those rheumy eyes, the game knee, the bad hip, or whatever—Frankie, the fastest kid in eighth grade. Frankie, basketball hero of the victory over St. Ambrose. Frankie, who'd survived that terrible brawl in Pusan, never deserting his buddies though the odds were five to one.

"Where does he get the letters?"

"At the parish office."

"Really. From whom?"

She shrugged. "I don't know. The parish secretary?"

"Who's in charge over there?"

"Reverend Jenkins."

"What do you know about him?"

"He's been pastor at St. Paul for twenty years."

"How long has your dad been a parishioner?"

"Since he got religion again. Maybe seven, eight years."

I looked through the stack. "Why doesn't she write him at his address?"

"I asked Dad that. She said she's a single woman and feels more comfortable writing through the mission."

This had all the earmarks of a scam. Because it *was* a scam. Some lousy shithead was taking advantage of an old man's trusting heart. I felt a strong buzz in my fist.

"What do you think, Mr. Henry?"

"I think someone is taking your dad to the cleaners."

"What do I do?"

"Depends on what's more important to you." I raised a hand in warning. "I mean no disrespect. But what's more important? Dad's money or his heart?"

"What do *you* mean?"

"Your dad is seventy-eight. When did your mother pass?"

"How did you know?"

"I bet as long as your mom was around your dad never set foot in church. Am I right?"

Betty nodded. A choked silence followed. "She died . . . ten years ago."

I handed her a napkin. Again I was reminded that all of us had suffered terrible blows, that we were the walking wounded. Fractured, crushed, punctured, abraded, lacerated. The five categories of injury.

After a bit Betty took a deep breath and apologized. "So what do I do, Mr. Henry?"

"Money is just money. As long as you have enough. Only you would know what that sum means to your dad. On the other hand, at a time in his life where he probably thought that love was beyond him, suddenly there it is."

"Here it is."

"So it's up to you. Break his heart, shatter his pride, make him feel like a fool, and maybe this asshole will get a slap on the wrist. If we're lucky. Maybe he'll plead out to a misdemeanor, get fined, and he'll have to make restitution. A hundred dollars a month for the next ten years."

"Dad won't live that long."

"And every check he'll get will remind him he was a goddam fool." Like Lynette reminded me I was goddam fool.

"What's the alternative?" Betty clenched her fists in rage. "This bastard should die."

"That may be what he deserves. But that's not what I do, and that's not what you do. But he will have to clean up his mess."

"How do you know it's a he?"

"This sort of scam is not usually a woman's crime. Not usually."

"How does he clean up the mess?"

"Francie must die."

CHAPTER SIXTEEN

Jerry Shunk

Unless a person is professionally aware of the arts of surveillance he is oblivious to its practice. I decided to set my Laurel Canyon Irregulars on Lynette's trail to see what she was all about. Besides Dick Henry.

I didn't pay the Irregulars much, just enough to keep them in marijuana and gasoline. But they were young, willing, and digital. Four days later I had a thousand images to sort through on my laptop.

Lynette, I could not call her Judy, rose late and spent the day spending money. When she got up at all. Eating, shopping, hanging with friends. She had three automobiles to choose from. She was no stewardess.

Looking through the cache, I saw there was an older man who didn't fit into the friendship demographic. They'd met twice. Bistro Bijou on Ventura, and in Santa Monica on the Third Street Promenade. All in all, I had forty or so pictures of them. Every angle. Never intimate. God, she was gorgeous. I anesthetized a red thread of jealousy with some nicotine.

The man was tall, skinny, sixty, well dressed. But his hair. Jesus. At least it wasn't a comb-over. It had been dyed a pastel blue, curled tightly and permed, making the best of a volume shortage. A potbelly lumped abruptly over his belt line.

Then I recognized him. Shunk. Jerry Shunk.

Shunk was a family law practitioner whose largely ancient clientele always found ways to drop dead and leave him everything.

A scenario played out in my mind. Eternally grateful after getting screwed right and left during the term of their marriage, Artie would die suddenly and conveniently, leaving Lynette everything. And part of everything would go to Jerry Shunk. Who was plainly lovesick. A vibration that usually, when obvious, drives a woman away faster than shoes of man-made materials. But there she was. Yes, the attraction had to be legal.

Didn't it?

CHAPTER SEVENTEEN

What Makes Us Human

A couple of nights later there was a knock at my door.

In the cold light of past mornings I'd planned on giving her the heave-ho but then she laughed in that certain way and I wanted her. She kissed me and emotion triumphed over intellect.

Part of emotion over intellect lies in the mechanics of natural selection. If we came from long lines of cold-blooded rationalists, *we* would be cold-blooded rationalists. But we're not, and emotional primacy has to be part of why our species is successful. The fact that all of us, from the president of the United States à la Monica to the president of your one-man hot dog stand, place heart over head implies that, from the haze of prehistory, those who placed heart above head were more successful than their logical competitors.

Which means there's something to be said for the damn-the-torpedoes approach; that, in fact, the statistical consequences of emotional decisions are more positive than negative. Perhaps emotion is intellectual shorthand.

In other words, if it feels good, it probably *is* good. Which reminds me of what David Lee Roth said about music the night I met Lynette at the House of Blues. What's good music, Dave? Well, if it sounds good, it *is* good. Which Diamond

Dave may have learned from Bach because Bach said the same thing. And you thought they had nothing in common. Oscar Wilde on how to overcome temptation? Succumb.

So Lynette kissed me, and next thing I knew we were enjoying postcoital tobacco and crickets out my window.

"You know, Dick, I may be falling in love with you."

Bullshit. "Yeah?"

"Yeah."

What is love? With my little ones I know.

Who does Daddy love?

Me!

Why does Daddy love you?

Because he does!

Because I do. The only satisfactory answer to the love question. Not based on merit, not based on qualification. A simple recognition of your loved one's inherent pleasingness.

And romantic love? I don't know what it is anymore. Maybe I never did. Is it that glorious attention that confers grace, that shyness and openness that admit your power to delight? That perfectly spherical satisfaction of wishing to be nowhere else? That self-evident groove? The conspiracy of two against the universe?

Maybe it's all these things, maybe none of them. Whatever it is, as the days settled in after the Revelation, Lynette and I had it in full measure. We had a new laughter, a new clarity. The knowledge that after all that had transpired we still enjoyed each other's company very, very much. And now we had nothing to hide, right?

Of course it couldn't last, but singly and together we allowed that fact to recede into the background. We asked no more questions, we lived in our own universe, in our own time, Artie Benjamin rendered distant and inconsequential.

CHAPTER EIGHTEEN

Ojai

In the darkness I asked her if she'd ever been to Ojai and she said where's that so up we went.

Ojai is about seventy-five miles north of L.A. and there're two ways to go but I always liked the back way. Up the I-5 past Magic Mountain, then over on the 126 through the Santa Clara River Valley. The valley is lush and expansive, restful and satisfying to the eye, and the change from the scenery of the I-5 corridor startling.

"Wow."

I nodded. That's the kind of place the Santa Clara Valley was. If you looked to the ridge of the mountains to the south you could see oak trees here and there. How pleasant it would be to sit at their feet in a breeze.

"Those are oak trees up there, aren't they?"

"Those are the Oakridge Mountains." My geographical knowledge of the area was shallow and with that pronouncement I had dispensed half of it. "I think."

She jumped on me. "You *think*? You mean they could be any old mountains?"

"You see those oaks up there?"

"Maybe they're willows."

"Those are oaks. Those are the Oakridge Mountains."

"If you say so."

"Well, I think they are."

We laughed and laughed, and she put her hand on my leg. She looked north of the road, over the orange groves. "And what mountains are those?"

"That's easy. Those are the San Cayetanos."

"Sure about that?"

"Of course." I paused. "I think."

We laughed again. We passed a couple of fruit stands. I promised we'd stop on the way back. Next was the town of Fillmore. We parked beside the green, wandered among the trains, tasted wine from a winery along the tracks.

"Who lives here?" she asked.

I didn't know but it looked like a good life. A quiet life. A very quiet life.

Ten minutes later we arrived in Santa Paula and turned up Highway 150, Ojai Road.

Ojai Road was a two-lane thoroughfare that quickly left Santa Paula behind and entered the mountains. There it turned magical. It swooped, it dashed, it dipped, it sashayed. Then it climbed, slowly but inexorably, past single-family homes, past ranches and horse farms and schools, finally reaching a plateau where cattle grazed on vast fields of gold under wide open skies.

"Those cows," said Lynette, pointing.

"What about 'em?"

"Look at them."

"I'm looking."

"They look contented."

We laughed again.

She looked over at me. "I'm contented, Dick."

"So am I, dear." I indicated the fields. "Want to stop, grab ourselves a little hay?" The L.A.-ness of our lives had completely dropped away.

Then the road turned right, and huge, majestic, layered mountains appeared far away, dead ahead. "Those are the Topa Topas," I explained. And then, for a second, as the road suddenly started to serpentine downward, we had a view of a beautiful valley far below. "That's the Ojai Valley."

Shangri-la. The Lost World.

Slowly we dropped down, rolled into town.

We parked along the arcade, wandered in and out of stores, purchased trinkets and held hands. I was as happy as I'd ever been since seventh grade. We had pizza and wine at a good little place called Movino, and I got a little sleepy so we got a motel. A nice place, further on up the Ojai Road. I hadn't intended on staying the night but the sun was on the fall and what the hell.

We made lazy love and dozed until evening. Then we found a bistro with a piano player and decided to have dinner. During our second set of Bloody Marys she tapped me on the arm.

I looked at her. "You know you're absolutely gorgeous. You know that, right?"

She nodded. "I do know that."

I spread my hands. "Just so you know *I* know."

She pointed to the musicians. A stand-up bassist and a guitarist had joined the piano player. "How do you know if someone's really good," she asked, "or if they're just fooling around? You know, when they jam."

An alarm bell rang in my mind.

"Uhhh, it's a matter of something called tipping in. That's where a player uses certain notes in his improvisation that reflect the chords he's playing over."

"Sounds like you know a lot about jazz, Dick."

Unconsciously and beyond my control, my voice dropped a manly octave and before I could stop myself I'd given her a little rundown on vertical and horizontal improvisation. As I explained, the difference between bebop Charlie Parker and cool Miles Davis.

"Jeez, Dick. You really do know a lot about jazz."

I shook my head. "No. I don't."

"But you do." She polished off her second Bloody Mary and I followed suit. "Now what was that thing you mentioned that they do, *sitting in?*"

"No. That's when you're invited to come and blow a few tunes with the band." *Blow a few tunes.* Why was I talking like that? "You're talking about *tipping in.* That's using certain notes in your improv that are important notes in the chords you're jamming over. That lets the players know you know what you're doing."

She nodded. "I'd like to hear a little of that. That tipping in. What's a good tune for that?"

For crying out loud.

I ran my fingers through my hair. I only could remember the one. "Actually, there's a famous tune called 'All the Things You Are.' They say if you can jam on those changes you can call yourself a jazz musician."

"Righteous."

I stared at her. "Did we ever talk about this stuff before?"

"No." She took a sip from our third round. "I didn't think you knew anything."

We munched our way through the pupu platter, and the set ended.

"Dick," she said. "Ask these guys to play that tune."

"What tune?"

"The tipping-in tune."

"No."

"Why not?"

"I don't want to ask them."

"Why not?"

"Look. I just don't want to. Let's leave it at that."

Of course, she wouldn't take no for an answer.

When a pretty girl gives you a compliment you accept it with grace. When a startlingly beautiful girl strews compliments you believe her. In a trice she had the three believers by the short and curlies.

"Can we play a tune for you?" asked the piano player.

"Would you?"

Of course, said the bassist, the pianist, and the guitarist. What would she like to hear?

She looked up at me. "My boyfriend knows a lot about jazz but he's too shy to ask."

The trio rallied to her aid. Just name it, dude. Don't be bashful. We can even play in five-four time.

Jesus Christ.

"Okay, all right. Can you play, uh, 'All the Things You Are'?"

Their faces went stony and I knew what was coming. "We just played it, man," said the guitarist, plosively expelling a shred of tobacco.

Lynette turned and stared at me. Then broke out into peals of ascending laughter. It was contagious. I started off and couldn't stop. Then the bassist rolled in and soon the band was gone. We couldn't stand after a while but by then the three tables in front were with us, by osmosis.

After a bit we wiped our eyes, found our seats. Dinner was served. The band started in but not before announcing they had a special request for "All the Things You Are." Which started everyone laughing again and they couldn't play.

But finally they did. They played very crisply, very well. There was some good applause. Lynette looked over at me. "Well?"

"Well, what?"

"Was that the tune?"

I shrugged. "I don't know."

Lynette went off again and couldn't stop. The maître d' came to inquire if there were a problem. With the nitrous oxide.

"Can we just get this stuff to go?" I asked. Our request was swiftly satisfied, but before we left we went up to the bandstand and I gave the guys a honeybee.

They shook their heads. You don't have to do that.

"Oh, but I do," I replied. "This has been one of the great nights of my life."

And I promise it won't happen a third time.

One day turned into two, into four. It was paradise. We ate when we were hungry, we drank when we were dry, we made love and it was always new, and we slept, untroubled, like children. My phone didn't ring because I'd turned it off, just checked my messages. Nothing important.

On the fourth day we'd awoken late. We walked outside, considered the pool, but the day was too nice. In fact, it was perfect. Warm, quiet, wind chimes somewhere, their volume fluctuating in the light breeze. We decided to take a walk.

We wandered up into the streets behind the arcade. It was residential. Sizable houses on well-proportioned lots. After a few blocks and some random turns we came to an open house. It was a squarish, two-story Craftsman, olive green with brown trim. It had a brown picket fence to match, a straight brick walk, some tall trees, jacaranda and camphor, spreading over a clipped green lawn. "Nice place," I said.

"Let's go in."

We opened the screen door and stepped inside. It was cool and clean with shiny, light-colored hardwood flooring. There was no furniture. A broad staircase with a landing led upstairs. We heard a chair scrape in the kitchen, and a well-dressed, middle-aged woman walked out. She was all in beige except for white pumps. She stuck out her hand. "I'm Miriam Walters," she said. "Welcome."

We introduced ourselves. Dick and Lynette.

Are you interested in Ojai real estate?

Well, we're visitors and we were taking a walk and here we are.

"That's where it all starts. Let me show you around. You're my first guests of the day and I was getting lonely back there."

It was a five-bedroom place with a dining room, a living room, and a den, which could serve as our home office. The kitchen was big, with a slate double-sink island and a pair of Jenn-Airs venting into shiny ductwork. It made me want to cook.

Upstairs was a master suite, fireplace, walk-in closets, Jacuzzi bathtub. Then another two bedrooms, white, airy, with large black ceiling fans.

Then Mrs. Walters delivered the coup de grâce. "And here"—she smiled a brilliant smile—"is the nursery suite."

The nursery suite was white, but the walls and ceiling were a friendly riot of detailed murals. Tail-hanging monkeys smiled, elephants danced, birds soared, dolphins leapt from blue waves. Ships plied calm seas, gaily uniformed polemen maneuvered gondolas in Venice, overhead whirled the stars and galaxies of the infinite wheel.

"Wow." It was hard not to be impressed.

"Isn't it wonderful?" furthered Mrs. Walters. "All we need is a baby."

I heard a quick intake of breath from Lynette. I turned. She was frozen. She stared at me, almost violently, her eyes filled with tears.

"Lynette?"

She spun, walked right past me, down the stairs and out into the street.

"My God! Did I say something wrong?" asked Mrs. Walters. "I'm so sorry."

I ran down and out into the street, caught up with her. I reached for her arm but she shook me off.

I tried again. "Lynette, what? What is it?"

She spun on me fiercely, raw. "Don't you know when something's over, Dick? Don't you know when something's over?"

That was the end of our enchantment in Ojai. We checked out of paradise an hour later and drove back, in silence, back the way we had come. We didn't stop at the fruit stands.

The specter of Artie Benjamin arose with the tangled traffic on the I-5. I could feel him, gray, heavy, looming. We got back to Laurel Canyon and slept. We woke up, made quick remedial love, fell back.

I woke later in the dark. Three A.M. She was awake, lying on her back, smoking, a red point moving in the darkness. I remembered the sniper's maxim: *four inches above the red dot.* Aim four inches above the red dot. Which, in this case, would put a hole in the headboard.

"Hi, Dick." She sounded distant and fragile.

"Hi."

"I'm sorry. About all that."

"It's okay." It was cold. I asked her to shut the window and she did.

I thought of the stars on the ceiling of the nursery. The tiny spark of light that a consciousness injects into the unthinkable wastes of time and distance. As a man, I realized, I had never considered, even for an instant, the carrying of life within me. That visceral, literal connection to infinity, the propinquity of God. God Herself. I was a leaf that would have my spring, she was part of the tree that would reach for heaven. Except she wouldn't, couldn't.

Whew. Whatever it was she was feeling, I'd never get there. Maybe I could think of something practical. To distract things. "So what's your plan?"

"What plan are you talking about?"

"The future. What are you going to do?" I don't know what I was expecting.

There was a silence. Then she exhaled quickly, rolled over, ground the cigarette out.

"Why's my future your business? You want to get married or something?" Her voice was unpleasant.

"Just asking a question."

"Well, don't ask me questions. Do I ask you questions?" She sat up, got up. "I don't have a future." She stepped into her jeans.

If I'd used my brains, I would've just shut up. Because you can't argue your way out of an argument. With a woman, certainly. But who said I had any brains? "What's up *your* ass?" I inquired cleverly. "I thought people were pleasant after orgasm."

"Maybe I was faking."

"No, you weren't."

"How would you know?"

Actually a good question. The theatrical orgasm had a long, rich history. Back to the Garden of Eden. When Adam was a pest on Saturday night. With *I Love Lucy* coming on.

Two minutes later she was out the door.

CHAPTER NINETEEN

Subtlety and Patience

The next day was Blue Monday, so I rolled south down Vine Street toward my old house and the remnants of my old life. Right below Melrose, on the poor-relations outskirts of Hancock Park, I pulled to a stop at a small, three-bedroom Craftsman on South Arden Boulevard. I rang the doorbell and waited.

Georgette must have known it was me because she took her time about it. But then the big oak door was pulled back and there she was through the screen.

Georgette was a good-looking woman. She was Irish-German, a strawberry blonde. She was no twig; she hadn't weighed 105 pounds since grade school. She stood five feet eight, had big, well-shaped legs and a waist shadowed by a mud wrestler's generous bust.

She did not appear overly pleased to see me, overlooking my friendly smile. "What do you want, Dick?"

"I want to come in."

"Are you bringing money?"

"I am." Alimony and child support. Blue Monday.

"Come in."

I followed her down the hall. In that second, part of me desperately missed the regard in which I had been held. We could have gone all the way but I was Dick Henry after all and a small man casts that long shadow near sundown and I wanted what I wanted when I wanted it.

Georgette poured me a cup of coffee and I sat down at the kitchen table I had purchased so long ago. Oak.

I'd always liked Georgette's coffee. It was robust, like her chest. I set down my mug. "So, how've you been?"

"I've been okay, Dick." Uninflected and perfunctory.

"And how are my little people?"

"They're all right, too." A silence in the expectation that I would move along.

I grinned at her. "I almost forgot why I was here."

"Money."

"Money, that's right." I pulled out my checkbook, wrote two checks, signed them largely, handed them to her. "Here you go."

She took them, examined them, put them under the salt-shaker. "Why don't you just put these in the mail like other men do?"

I summoned all my charm. "Obviously, my dear, because I am not like other men."

"I try to explain that to your children."

"They'll have a lifetime to appreciate me." I smiled another sunny smile. "Actually, I like to see you once in a time."

Georgette frowned, exasperated. "What are you talking about?"

"You asked me a question, dear."

"I'm not your *dear*, Dick. What question did I ask?"

"Why don't I put them in the mail like other men do?"

"Well, what about it?"

"Because I like to see you once in a while. That's why I don't put the check in the mail."

A pinkness rose in Georgette's cheeks. Which pleased me greatly.

I placed a paper bag on the table, took out a stack of books. "These are for Randy. First half of the Edgar Rice Burroughs Mars series. The best books I ever read as a kid."

Georgette picked up *The Warlord of Mars*. On the cover, a well-built man, dressed only in a scabbard, defended a statuesque, copper-skinned woman against a great white ape with two sets of arms. "Randy's only eleven."

"That's why I got them."

Georgette sighed—but moved the books to her side of the table.

I looked at Georgette. She was checking out the man in the scabbard. "So, you want to go down to the Galley and grab ourselves a lobster one of these nights?"

It took Georgette a few seconds to remember she didn't like me anymore. "No! Are you crazy, Dick?"

As I drove up Vine Street later, I felt a general optimism flow through my bones. Georgette still loved me. I could see it in everything she did. The way she moved, her attitude, her speech.

Because there's only one Dick Henry in this world and that's me, baby. Georgette would come back around. In time. If I was extremely subtle and patient. And I am extremely subtle and patient.

I rolled into the intersection at Vine and Santa Monica on the new red and banged a left to a clamor of horns from everywhere. Get a life.

CHAPTER TWENTY

A Photograph

I'd done a little thinking about the letters to Franklin Tillman. The source of the evil had to be somewhere at St. Paul of Tarsus.

How does someone start a conversation with someone who doesn't exist? Well, they must be convinced that someone *does* exist. Which means a long story or a picture. A long story pointed to premeditation and careful choice of victim. Which made it unlikely. No, it started with a picture.

A legitimate photo of the mission staff. In that photo, by coincidence, would have been a friendly face, an attractive woman from her forties to her sixties. Smiling and waving, like everyone else.

Tillman would've seen the picture. Probably everyone at St. Paul had seen the picture. But Tillman had made a remark to somebody. Someone who had the photo in their hands. Someone who said, *Yes, she's very pretty.*

She looks so sweet, said Tillman.

And that statement, in the hands of the right person, was the seed of opportunity. So the old widower was prompted. *Why don't you write her, Franklin? Her name is . . . Francie.*

No. I couldn't.

Why not?
I could do that?
Of course you could.
She wouldn't think I was out of line?
Why should she? You both love the Lord.
You're sure I wouldn't be out of line?
We'll send it over in the weekly mission package.
You could do that?
Of course we could.
Then maybe I will write her a letter.
It's up to you.
Then I will.
Go for it, Franklin.
I will. I just think I will.

CHAPTER TWENTY-ONE

Pumpkin Pie

What drove the final, final nail into Georgette and me was Kiera Allen's pumpkin pie.

Swept along by Kiera's mirage of intelligence and kindness, qualities I had lent her, our relationship acquired an ungainly momentum of its own. To my surprise, the sex wasn't that good though we cried out and swore. Her passion seemed histrionic. Her apartment was full of mirrors and she seemed to be eyeing herself in the third person.

We went on long expeditions to nowhere, to outlet malls in Camarillo and Barstow and Colton. Even there, in the sun-baked wastelands far from civilization, at every turn I expected to see my mother-in-law.

In Barstow, at Salon 212, where leathery desert rats, at desert prices, could purchase chic apparel supposedly of New York City lineage, Kiera finally found something she liked. "Dick, what do you think?"

I turned to regard a long, red-orange, zebra-skin coat. If such a beast had ever existed, it had grazed the Serengeti unmolested.

That evening, in her apartment crowded with stuffed animals and other cute stuff, she looked soulfully into my eyes.

Suddenly, my fervent hope was that a declaration of love would not be forthcoming.

"I need you, Dick," she said as the sweat dried on our skin.

Shit. Here it came. "Okay."

"Oh, yes," she replied solemnly. "Or someone just like you."

Part of me was stupid enough to feel insulted. But in the end it didn't matter. Kiera Allen, femme fatale, had turned back into a very ordinary woman. I heard her voice echoing off the pink bathroom tiles. "Dick? Dick?"

"What?"

"Dick?"

"*What?*"

"Dick, I think I've got a yeast infection."

For chrissakes.

The end came on Thanksgiving Day. For obvious reasons, I told her not to expect me, certainly not to call me. Did I have to explain further? But I received an emergency call on my business line.

Be back in an hour, I told Georgette. The smell of turkey was in the air, and even Estelle, my mother-in-law, had swilled an early glass of chardonnay.

Kiera met me at the door in a little French maid's outfit with fishnet stockings and a flouncy apron. Before I could protest, her tongue was down my throat. She pulled my hands onto her ass, then reached into my trousers and had her way with me.

"I thought you said there was an emergency."

"I needed you in my mouth," she said.

A whole Thanksgiving meal had been laid out. Turkey, glazed ham, stuffing, sweet potatoes with melted marshmallows, cranberry sauce, mashed potatoes, buttered corn, asparagus, red and white wine. And a pumpkin pie.

The turkey was very, very bland. "It's a certified organic turkey," said Kiera, with a big, simpering smile.

A certified organic turkey. Great. It had probably been bored to death instead of just having its head cut off.

"Just think," said Kiera, "our first Thanksgiving."

That's when I saw the clock. Somehow just a bite had already taken an hour and ten minutes.

Now I raced down the street with a heaping plate covered in Saran Wrap. Where was a homeless psychiatrist or mathematician when you needed one? I threw the plate into a trash can at the bus stop. It landed with a thud.

I arrived home two hours seventeen minutes after I'd left.

"Where were you?" asked Georgette, looking up from the feast in progress. Estelle's face had that pinched expression that came with the giving of unsolicited advice. Georgette's sister, Bay, and her husband, Trout, looked up at me quizzically. Okay, his name was Trent. But all the kids were glad to see Uncle Dick.

"Sorry. Business," I lied, with enthusiasm. "Make me up a plate."

I tried to eat but I was full already. I picked and poked but it was slow going. I loosened my belt and thought of famished predators on the Serengeti.

"Aren't you hungry, Dick?" asked Georgette.

"My, uh, stomach's a little off, I guess." I rubbed it. It felt as hard as a basketball. I shoehorned another carrot down my throat and gulletized a small spear of asparagus.

Then the doorbell rang.

Curious faces around the table.

"Now who could that be?" asked Estelle disagreeably.

Obviously she had forgotten the Prada purse I'd bought her for her 179th birthday. Albeit from Santee Alley, downtown L.A.'s haven of counterfeit merchandise.

Georgette got up and walked to the door to find out what was up.

Estelle looked at my plate. "Why aren't you hungry?"

I shrugged.

Georgette returned. Her face was several degrees below freezing.

"Who is it, Georgie?" asked Estelle.

Georgette turned to me. Just like in the movies, there was a pregnant pause.

"What is it?" I asked, suddenly intuiting disaster.

"You have a visitor."

"A visitor?" said Estelle. "What kind of visitor?"

I pushed my chair back, got up, went to the front door, pulled it open.

On the other side of the screen door was a woman in an orange zebra-skin coat. Kiera was very drunk. She proffered another Saran-Wrapped plate. A rumpled slice of pumpkin pie. "Di-ick," she said.

"What the fuck?"

"Di-ick. You forgot your pumpkin pie."

CHAPTER TWENTY-TWO

Afternoon at the Fellatio Academy

Benjamin Enterprises had offices in Beverly Hills, on Beverly Drive below Wilshire in a colonial-looking building. The free-parking structure was full so I had to cruise a back street.

I found a spot near the corner. Well, two spots, but a silvery Korean import was in both of them. This was no problem if you owned a '69 Cadillac Coupe de Ville convertible. I pulled in front of Pusan's finest, backed up carefully until I kissed it, then, with 472 cubic inches of raw Detroit horsepower, pushed it back and created my parking place. You gotta know how to use your Cadillac.

Benjamin's offices were cool and subdued. I was greeted by a secretary. "Will Mr. Benjamin know the purpose of your visit?"

"Yes," I said, leaving her curiosity unsatisfied. On the wall I saw a poster for *Arm Service*. Then, partially obscured by a potted plant, a larger poster for *Buffalo Bill in Hollywood*.

Suddenly, over the quiet, I heard a voice raised in anger. It was Benjamin.

"Listen, motherfucker, you tell that stupid son of a bitch to straighten up and fly right. Nobody fucks with Artie Benjamin and dances off into the fuckin' sunset, you got that? Now call me back when it's done."

I heard the phone slam down and wondered, for the fortieth time, what was Benjamin's real game? What did he really know? Why was I really here? I didn't know, couldn't know. I'd have to bluff it out.

Benjamin's Filipino appeared. He still didn't like me. Maybe he didn't like anyone. I'd have to ask Lynette about him.

"Mr. B will see you."

I followed him back. He took his place, standing by Benjamin's left side.

Benjamin was behind another huge desk. He looked at me, grinned. "I just had a brainstorm. A fucking brainstorm," he began, "about school."

"School?"

He pointed at me, grinned. "See? That's exactly what I mean. I say "school" and people think, What the fuck does Artie Benjamin know about school? What does he *care* about school?"

I nodded politely in agreement. To my knowledge, no one gave a fuck what Artie Benjamin thought about anything.

"To those who know, your name does not exactly bring up scholarship," I said carefully. But then I made the inductive leap. "Unless you're thinking about *schoolgirls*." In those little plaid uniforms. And white kneesocks. And little white panties.

Benjamin slapped his desk. "You got it! You got it! What do you think of this?" He raised his arms, spread his hands, imagining a marquee. "Artie Benjamin presents—*The Fellatio Academy*! Get it? *The Fellatio Academy*."

"A school for Italian diplomats," I returned.

Benjamin laughed aloud. "Maybe you *should be* an associate producer. What do you think?"

"Producers are about money. And I don't have any."

I'd been invited to a porn set once. And I'd accepted, you know, just to see. It was a regular house up Beverly Glen. There was a small technical crew. A buffet had been set up in the kitchen. The stars walked around naked, unembarrassed. Picking up a slice of pepperoni here, a cheese ball there.

Action was cold-blooded sex on cue. Every unobstructed orifice, with the exception of the nostril and the ear canal, was stuffed and pounded relentlessly, the eye of the camera six inches away from the organs involved. The women feigned perpetual orgasm, pleaded for more. The men had finite limits and would signal the camera operator when the money shot approached. Then they would disengage and ejaculate as directed. On the face, on the breasts, on the stomach, on the ass. But mostly on the face, where the tincture of humiliation was combined with epidermal rejuvenation.

If I'd been concerned about my own arousal and how to pretend disinterest, I needn't have worried. Without the fleeting, salutary fictions that had supported even my interactions with virtual strangers, the sex was sexless and I was profoundly unmoved.

The afternoon on Beverly Glen had an unintended consequence. My fantasy life disappeared. Whereas previously I had engaged in benign sexual speculation about every woman who appealed to me, now I looked upon the feminine form without hope or curiosity. As days turned to weeks I began to worry that I had damaged myself.

From sixteen to the occasional well-preserved Diane Keaton sixty, anyone might set me off. The sway in the walk, the sauciness of a laugh, the divine bounce of the natural bust. Twenty seconds later I'd see someone else and start over.

Then one day, when I had despaired of its return, it was back. A waitress bent to pour my coffee and I saw a dark freckle and part of me went *Look at that.* I left her an excellent tip.

* * *

Benjamin leaned his head, studied me. I put my bluff on.

"So, Mr. Henry. What can you tell me?"

I felt my heartbeat in my temples. "Unfortunately, Mr. Benjamin, your suspicions were well founded. Your wife was seeing someone." I had to say she was seeing somebody—deep down, he already knew it.

"Is or was?"

"Was."

He sat there a second. Then one word. "Okay."

He opened his desk, pulled out a Sig Sauer P250, placed it on his desk.

I didn't move a muscle. My heart didn't beat either.

Then he reached back into his desk. This time he came out with an envelope. I could feel the Filipino's eyes on me. Benjamin slid the envelope across the desk toward me.

"You said seven large?"

"That's what I said."

Benjamin nodded.

I got to my feet, picked up the envelope. "Thank you for your patronage, Mr. Benjamin."

His eyes flicked over me. There was the ghost of a nod.

I left.

I got the Caddy, drove down the street, made a U-turn, and headed for Hollywood. As I passed the place I had parked I saw a woman looking at her Daewoo in confusion. Had her automobile moved?

I chortled. With joy and relief. I had seven thousand dollars in my pocket. I felt brilliantly alive.

Don't fuck with the Motor City, Daewoo lady. Just don't do it.

CHAPTER TWENTY-THREE

Arnuldo's Tale

Arnuldo Guinaldo had journeyed far from Tondo, the poorest, meanest, dirtiest, most desperate district in the city of Manila. Home to half a million hardened souls, tempered in strife, quenched in misfortune. He had never known his father. Nor did his mother remember. Most likely his father had been an American airman stationed at Nichols Air Force Base.

His education had been limited to the basics. The nuns ensured that he could read, that he could write, that he could do sums. But he possessed certain qualities older men could clearly identify. He had no fear and he had no conscience.

This lack stood him well in Tondo. At age twelve, after his mother died with the needle still stuck in her median cephalic vein, he had sought out the man who sold her the heroin and butchered him.

With the heroin man's little bit of money, he made his way to Olongapo City, Disneyland of the Seventh Fleet, where his mother had mentioned a sister. He never found her. But he did find gainful employment in Olongapo's largest industry, prostitution. He ferried drugs for the girls and the American sailors they lay with and performed a thousand other useful tasks. Like securing fresh chicken blood for the professional virgins, that they might prove their innocence weekly and finally capture a sailor for a husband. To catch a husband was to catch the rainbow and ride it to the USA.

Four years later, behind the Solar Club, an establishment on Rizal Boulevard devoted exclusively to the music of Miles Davis, Arnuldo had saved Machinist's Mate Third Class Ed Dinkins from certain death.

A disagreement had arisen with four young savages hailing from the Jungle, part of Olongapo and strictly off-limits to Americans. Very high, and tipping toward violence, the four were demanding the American's money or the life of the whore with whom he'd been keeping company. Dinkins was very drunk and had not appreciated the gravity of his situation. He had turned his pockets inside out. He'd spent his last peso seeing an excellent Filipino rendition of Miles Davis in his *Silent Way* period. Dong Custodio was the best trumpet player in the Philippines. And who knew there was a Filipino Joe Zawinul? Well, there was. Alfonso Magat.

At Dinkins's side, Delia, his girlfriend, whose virginity he had taken just that afternoon, tried to reason with the young men.

The first of the four animals flicked out his butterfly knife and sliced Delia's cheek. Arnuldo heard her cry and something was loosed in his chest. He bounded across the intervening space and extinguished the lives of the four young men.

Two weeks later, Dinkins, twenty-two, married Delia at the Subic Bay Naval Station Multi-Purpose Center. Delia was not twenty, as advertised. She was a young-looking twenty-seven. She was very happy. The couple adopted Arnuldo. He was sixteen. Dinkins took them both back to paradise: Poway, California, USA.

Four years later Delia and Dinkins were dead. Arnuldo followed a dancer to Las Vegas. The dancer was a whore and he killed her. But the climate agreed with him.

He had become part of Mr. Benjamin's life during Mister's first extended stay in Las Vegas.

In a bar at Caesars Palace, Arnuldo had offered the man the funniest joke he'd ever heard. Besides the one about the old couple on the night of their fortieth anniversary. And the see-through gown. Where the ancient husband had succeeded.

"What do you call a boomerang that does not come back?" asked Arnuldo.

Mr. Benjamin, on his second double Stoli, came up empty, lifted his shoulders. "What *do* you call a boomerang that does not come back?"

"A stick," said Arnuldo, on his third Bloody Mary, choking.

To Arnuldo's delight, Mr. Benjamin also found the jest irresistible. After another double Stoli Mr. Benjamin offered Arnuldo a job.

CHAPTER TWENTY-FOUR

Filthy Heat

Lynette came over the next night. We screwed, quickly and violently, then set to argument.

Which played into my new theory. The equivalence of sex and argument.

Any couple possesses a natural level of intimacy, a function of personality. Unconsciously, the couple seeks to maintain that intimacy. Some couples screw. Others argue.

My point, which Lynette had led me to consider: is there really a difference?

There's an inciting incident, a climb to passion, a climax, then all quiet on the Western Front. Though, admittedly, there's less chance your partner will whip up a little Spanish omelet after being called a mindless clam.

The subject of the argument was Artie.

She glared at me. "If he ever finds out, he's going to kill you."

"Why hasn't he killed *you* already?"

"Because to forgive me is to feel like a god."

"Well, God just paid me. The situation's over."

"Paid you to sell me out."

"*Sell you out?* Fuck you for that."

"You said what you said, Dick."

"I told him what he already knew, dear. This isn't my first fucking case." I jabbed my finger at her. "And it isn't your first case, either."

She snorted, jabbed her cigarette back at me. "This is one of those situations in life called opportunity, Dick. But you have to have the guts to grab it for what it is."

"Give it up, Lynette. I can't be shamed into murder."

"You know what he did to my sister."

"Yeah."

"You know the whole story?"

"Part of it." Supposedly Nyla Darkly, a.k.a. Thirsty Thelma, had been her sister.

"Which part?"

"The part where you don't have a sister." According to Myron Ealing's *Encyclopedia of Pornography,* Nyla Darkly had no sister. Her real name was Elizabeth Gligg. "You're a pretty bad liar, too."

With that, I engendered a second climb to passion. She came at me in a rage, claws out, ready to bite, to damage, but I was too strong for her. A knee came for my balls but I turned and her knee slid up my hip. We held each other close, wrestling.

"I'm going to kill you . . . one day."

"I thought it was Artie."

"I'll get my chance."

"No, darling. You won't."

She tried to bite me but couldn't, and pretty soon it was almost a vicious kiss and then it was a kiss. We separated and stared at one another.

A complete stranger. I didn't know her from Adam. A face from the supermarket, from the gas station, from the crossing gate, in the night, in another vehicle, waiting for that thousand-car train to roll through. "I don't know who you are, lady."

She cocked her head. "Yeah?" She waited a beat, then hauled off and slapped me right across the face. I put my hand to the sting.

Now I remembered.

I slapped her right back just as hard, knocking her head back. It was certainly not the way to treat somebody's wife.

But the vibe had changed. A filthy heat coursed through my veins. I grabbed her blouse and ripped it right off.

CHAPTER TWENTY-FIVE

A Contract

It was midnight. Her scent persisted on my skin. They say those who walk the delicate edge secretly hope to fall. But into what? I showered, poured peroxide over my scratches.

The phone rang. I answered on the fourth ring. It would be Lynette, of course. Urging me, again, to take out Benjamin. For my own good. For money after probate.

It was Benjamin.

"What can I do for you, Mr. Benjamin?" What had she done or said now?

"Mr. Henry. When we first talked I said that knowing, just knowing one way or the other, would be enough for me."

"That's what you said. That's the information I gave you."

"Well, I've changed my mind."

"What do you want now?"

"I want more. I need a name, Mr. Henry."

"You're changing the nature of our agreement, Mr. Benjamin."

"I know that."

Sweet Christ.

"Mr. Henry, you there?"

"I'm here. But I don't like doing these things over the phone."

"Then come pay me a visit."

"You've changed the nature of our agreement, Mr. Benjamin."

"I change agreements all the time. This is Hollywood. Money talks, right? I've got another five large for you."

He thought I was holding out.

Okay. Okay. What to do. "I'll be right over."

I rolled west on Sunset. The product of lies is more lies, like cracks spreading through a windshield. Sooner or later you can't see.

He needed a name. He needed a name. *I* needed a name. My folks, God bless them, had always taught me to stand up and face the music. But I couldn't see the music being of much use to anyone in this case. And though, when I came to think of it, Chuckie Gregory of A-1 Contractors could use another drumming, somehow I felt that giving Benjamin his name would be transgressing too many lines of karma.

There was plenty of parking on Rexford. The Filipino let me in and led me up, took his customary place to Benjamin's left. This evening he added to his charm by pulling out a vicious butterfly knife, snapping it open—then cleaning his fingernails.

Benjamin rewarded the show with a lordly smile of acknowledgment. "You can go, Arnuldo."

Arnuldo bowed and disappeared.

Benjamin reached into his desk, pulled out an envelope, slid it across. "Five large."

"Five large." I slid the envelope into my pocket.

"So, tell me, Mr. Henry. What's this asshole's name?"

The name had occurred to me as I passed Miyagi's on the Strip. Miyagi's had been Preston Sturges's old place, The Players. Sturges had broken important rules in the movie business. *Writers don't direct.* He directed. That was good. Then he broke important rules in the restaurant business. *Don't have too many doors and don't hire your friends and relatives.* He had too many doors and hired too many friends and relatives. That was bad. He went broke.

Suddenly I'd craved a Bloody Mary with salt on the rim. And the name had come to me.

"Salt. His name is Tom Salt."

Benjamin nodded. "Tom Salt." He looked up at me. "Sounds a lot like your name."

"It does?" My heart pumped vapor. "If you say so."

Benjamin steepled his fingers. "I've always believed a man grows up to fully inhabit his given name. Dick Henry, Tom Salt. Tom Salt, Dick Henry. Small, ordinary names."

"Tom, Dick, and Henry."

Benjamin laughed, help up his hand. "No disrespect intended, of course. What I mean is, if your name is Thurston, or Peyton, or Winston, or Prescott, or one of those, you grow up to be a Thurston or a Prescott. Get it?"

Kinda.

"I'm not sure he knew that Judy was married." In defense of Salt.

"Fuck him. He should have known."

He should've indeed. Ignorance is no defense before the law or an angry husband. Benjamin rubbed his chin, looked at Dick.

"You know what I'm going to do?"

"Forgive him because he knows not what he does."

"Does?"

"Did."

"No forgiveness, Mr. Henry. No. I'm going to have him killed."

"*Killed?*" This was more than a crack in the windshield.

"I'm sorry, Mr. Henry."

Sorry? Here it came. I could feel Arnuldo's knife in my back. "Why are you sorry?"

"I didn't realize you'd want the job."

Sweet gentle Christ save the worthless skin of your lying son.

"You *do* want the job?"

"Uh-huh, of course I do."

"Wonderful. How much?"

I remembered dreams I'd had, terrible dreams of my car sliding into an impenetrable fog on a dangerous highway at night, knowing that the vehicle certain to kill me would suddenly be right in front of me and unavoidable.

"How much, Mr. Henry?"

I scratched my head as if thinking. "Fifty. Twenty-five down. Twenty-five on completion."

Benjamin nodded. "Cheaper than I'd thought."

"Package deal."

"How long does it take?"

"Uh, couple of weeks. End of next week."

"How will I know the job's been done?"

"His obituary in the *Times*."

Benjamin slapped his hand on his desk. "Great. Do him."

I held up my hand for time. "You realize, Mr. Benjamin, you're taking an extreme step. There's no turning back. And you may feel worse about it later than you do now. I really don't advise it." And perhaps you won't hire me to kill myself.

Benjamin nodded his head, then leaned forward. "You ever have money, Mr. Henry?"

"No." Nothing I was afraid to lose.

"I thought so. It's pretty disappointing. It can get you all sorts of pretty things, all kinds of them, but nothing of real value. And I'm resigned to the fact that I'll probably never have anything I really want. But lately I've become curious— about the taste of revenge."

He reached into his desk. He counted two banded stacks of hundreds and counted fifty off a third.

"About Tom Salt."

"Yes?"

Benjamin smiled coldly. "I don't care if he suffers."

That was good to know.

Of course, Benjamin didn't know shit about money. Because he'd always had it. To the average guy a lump of money could buy time. Time to think about the race you'd been running so hard and so long. Running downhill so fast you can't stop. Money conferred time to think. About what you could do with your life instead of just feeding your body, paycheck to paycheck, until it broke down, until it quit altogether.

Me, I had no time. Tomorrow would rush into next week, and by then I'd have to kill, convincingly, someone who'd never lived.

CHAPTER TWENTY-SIX

Soul Provider

I awoke the next morning, a seamless dread draped over my shoulders. A shroud of foreboding. I didn't want to think about what I'd have to accomplish to get Benjamin off my back.

I decided for lighter fare. The Betty Fraiden matter.

I'd pay a call at St. Paul of Tarsus. The parish secretary, a slightly built, dark-haired man of medium height, thirtyish, opened the door to my bell.

"Can I help you?"

"I'd like to see Reverend Jenkins."

"Do you have an appointment?"

Just my luck. Even the soul business had worldly protocols. "No, I don't have an appointment."

"No? Then—"

"But I feel my immortal soul is in peril. Is the reverend in?"

I guess it was hard to reject a direct appeal to his higher duties. I waited in the parlor as the secretary made inquiries within. I was ushered into a small room to wait.

I looked around. Was this the lair of a rogue priest? Not obviously. Over a bookcase hung a crucifix with a burnished brass Christ. On the wall were photos of an elderly man in a Roman collar with various celebrities I'd never heard of.

The same photos hung at Pink's Hot Dogs. Or at any dry cleaner you might patronize. C-list celebrities would hand out their pictures to Christ himself:

Hang in there, Jesus! Bert Marks
Jesus, you're a miracle! Link Darnell
Rock on, Jesus! Peter Hart
U B cool, Mr. Christ. T-bar Yusef
Jesus, you tell the best fish stories! Bing Cherry
Jesus, you really cross me up! Lettie Figgus

Then the door opened, and the man in the photographs walked in. Reverend Jenkins was tall, rubicund, big-boned yet fragile-looking, with a full shock of longish white hair topping the bill. He was in his seventies and the kindest looking man I'd ever seen.

"I've lost my keys," said the reverend first thing, rummaging through his pockets.

I stood up. He extended a big hand. "Stuart Jenkins."

"Dick Henry." In the same time it took to realize that Artie Benjamin's wife was unfaithful to her husband, I knew the reverend was not the letter writer. He had some Parkinson's going on. His hands shook.

Jenkins carefully lowered himself into a chair, then looked at me. Those old eyes, without judgment, peered right into my soul. "Are you well, Mr. Henry?" he asked.

Of course, I had not come on matters of soul, but that's where his question found home.

How was I? How should I know? I'd been avoiding the issue as long as I could remember. There was a right and wrong and I pretty much left it at that, fundamentally unexamined. Because if you dug too far, you'd know things, and then, if you had any conscience at all, you'd have to do something.

"I'm all right," I allowed. But suddenly the floor opened and I was thinking of Arthur.

My friend, my boon companion, my competition, my cheerful, befreckled coconspirator, fellow sharer of secret language. Our language. *Arthur!* My twin. The only person who simultaneously understood why Michael Thayer chasing another boy with a paper lunch bag full of water at recess in first grade was the funniest thing imaginable. *A bag of water!*

Arthur had turned back in the crosswalk for a colored pencil I'd dropped.

"Mr. Henry?"

I blinked into Reverend Jenkins's patience. "Actually, I just thought of my twin brother. Lost him a long time ago."

"I'm sorry to hear that."

"Do you, uh, do you think you might . . . mention him in a prayer or two?"

"I'd be happy to. What was his name?"

What *is* his name. "Arthur." From somewhere I felt a tiny wattage, his crinkly smile.

Though I had often mocked the professionally religious as keepers of Cadillacs and catamites, the vast majority of clerical foot soldiers were dedicated men. They visited the sick, comforted the dying, told uplifting stories to children, maintained their creaky, wobbly faiths to encourage others. Practices that left them little time for themselves. Reverend Jenkins was all that in spades. I decided I liked Reverend Jenkins immensely.

"You maintain a mission in the Philippines, right?"

"Actually, we Episcopalians have many. St. Thomas supports two in particular. One in Manila, one in Cebu. The island of Cebu."

"How does somebody donate to that mission in Manila?"

"That's all taken care of by our man out front, Michael Linscomb."

"Seems like a good man."

"Yes, indeed. Hard worker. Quiet. Keeps to himself. I think he's writing a novel. And he writes with both hands!" Jenkins smiled. "He's ambidextrous. I never understood how those people do that. He lives here on the property."

"He handles all the mission work?"

"Those are among the duties of a church secretary. He's our official liaison."

"Is that a well-paid position?"

Jenkins laughed. "He makes more than I do."

"I didn't mean to be nosy, Reverend."

"My reward is in the hands of my Father. And in the mirror every morning."

I stood up and put out my hand. "A pleasure to make your acquaintance, sir."

He rose, and we shook.

Then I saw his keys on the third shelf of the bookcase. "And there are your keys." I pointed.

His face lit up. "Of course. I was rereading some Aquinas." He raised a finger, "'Good can exist without evil, whereas evil cannot exist without good.'"

I raised a finger of my own. "'Love takes up where knowledge leaves off.'"

Where had that come from? Maybe it was the Jesuits. Loyola High. I was as surprised as Jenkins.

He laughed aloud. "I detect the presence of an altar boy."

I took leave of Reverend Jenkins with firmer step. Humanity could not disappoint me, as I expected nothing of it, but this afternoon I would be buoyed.

I passed Linscomb on my way out. I didn't like him. His dark eyes glittered. "May Christ be with you."

"Thank you." I got to the door, then turned back. "I need the address of the mission in Manila. Could you write that down for me, please?"

He hesitated a second, pulled out a sheet of paper, hesitated again. Was he choosing hands? Then, left-handed, he wrote down the address, handed it to me.

The Caddy drove south of its own accord. "Love takes up where knowledge leaves off." How had that quotation come to surface? I thought about Lynette and what I really knew about her.

Nothing.

And, yes, I had been an altar boy.

Two altar boys were helping Father Falvey on a Saturday morning. Confessions were being heard, and as young Tommy Mollet was pushing the dust mop around and giggling with Peter, Father Falvey stuck his head out of the confessor's box and beckoned the young man.

"I need you to take over for me, Tommy," said the priest. "I've got to take a monstrous crap."

A *crap*? Father Falvey sat at the right hand of God. He took craps? Monstrous ones? And even then, would he, Tommy Mollet, be allowed by church law to substitute for Father Falvey? He, Mollet, was a well-known sinner. And, as God knew only too well, he had called his sister a shitbird just this morning. And what would he say to the people confessing? How would he mete out punishment?

"But what do I say to them, Father?" Tommy was feeling overwhelmed.

"Just give them what I give you. A couple of Our Fathers and a Hail Mary or two. You'll get the hang of it."

Into the dark little room Tommy went, sat on a small bench against the wall. A little window was on each side, and each window had a sliding screen. To his horror, Tommy could clearly see the sinners when it came their time.

But he settled in after a while. Two Our Fathers, one Hail Mary. Three Our Fathers, five Hail Marys.

Then Patrick Gleason had come in. "Bless me, Father, for I have sinned. It's been a week since my last confession." Gleason confessed he had shat in the St. Vincent de Paul box.

Whoa. Even though he, Tommy Mollet, had laughed himself sick on the playground, from the confessional it was a different story. Ten Our Fathers, and ten Hail Marys. Then he added the stinger, "For three days."

A shadow entered and he smelled perfume. It was April Douglas. She had the largest breasts in class. She started in and very quickly Tommy felt way over his head. Quietly he opened the door, waggled his fingers at Peter.

"What?" whispered Peter. Why had Father chosen Tommy over him anyway? Tommy didn't know shit about shit.

Tommy, desperate, looked up at his friend. "What does Father Falvey give for oral and anal sex?" Whatever they were.

Peter shrugged. Why *had* Father chosen Tommy over him? "Simple. Two tickets to the Dodgers."

CHAPTER TWENTY-SEVEN

The Pharaoh's Raft

I rolled downtown. With Mr. Linscomb behind me, I was now going to need a dead man, so once again I resorted to my relationship with Billy Ravenich, whom I'd known from Navy days.

Ravenich and I had played in a blues band back then, Coalhouse Walker. Our dream had been punctured early on by lack of talent but it takes talent to see that. We ran on flat tires for a while and then they fell off.

Ravenich had gone on to actually do something in the music world. On some chart somewhere, he and his friends had been #9 with a bullet. Heavy rock with a satanic twist. Witch Hunt, that was the name. Or was it Sea Hunt?

In any case the Hunt had limped to a generally unlamented conclusion and Ravenich had gone into the family business. The mortuary business.

The O'Halloran Mortuary was on Venice approaching downtown. Freeways hummed overhead, and a merciless sun beat down on a mission-style paint job gone powdery. A sign on a telephone pole suggested a new credit identity might be had for forty-nine dollars.

Inside it was solemn, quiet, and well air-conditioned, a must for any mortuary; in the background a lugubrious organ grieved. I stepped on a threshold mat and a low bell rang in the back.

A woman appeared. She was dressed in black and walked slowly, hands folded in consternation. Pale, middle-aged, significantly overweight, dark hair up in bun, she wore an expression of deep and enduring sympathy. A slash of very red lipstick completed the scenario.

"I'm Mrs. Grimble," she said with an oily solicitude. "How may I help you today?"

I loathed her instantly and pitied Mr. Grimble should he exist. I imagined Mrs. Grimble at home, ground into the flattened couch, issuing orders, bleating complaints, stuffing her craw with soft candy.

I recalled my mother's passing and the hash Forest Lawn had made of it, attempting to sell me a golden sarcophagus when she had requested a pine box. It was amazing, galling; even in death you were a commodity with upgrade potential.

I decided I would have fun with Mrs. Grimble until she gave up and called for Ravenich.

Mrs. Grimble reclasped her hands and repeated her inquiry. "May I be of service, sir?"

Let's see. "I'm here on behalf of my uncle."

She gestured me to an uncluttered desk, bade me sit. I sat and sniffed loudly.

Mrs. Grimble reached into a drawer, removed some forms, a pen, and a box of Kleenex. She slid the tissues over to me.

"First things first. What is your name?"

"Richard Henry."

"Ri-chard Hen-ry. And your uncle's name, sir?"

I sniffed loudly and spun the wheel of fortune. "His name was Charles."

"Charles. Charles who?"

"Uncle Charles."

A humorless smile creased her face. I wondered how long she'd done this job. "And his last name, sir?"

"Don't you want his middle name?"

"Of course. What was it?"

"His full name was Charles Hobson Glurk."

"Glurk?"

An unusual name to be sure. I sniffed. "From the Pennsylvania Glurks."

"Glurk." She nodded dolorously and wrote something on the form. "And when did Mr. Glurk pass away?"

I sighed, the pain still damp and recent. "When the governor failed and the cable snapped and the safe fell from the crane and hit him in the head."

Mrs. Grimble managed another small smile. "I mean when, as in what date, when did he pass away?"

"The day before yesterday."

"And where is the deceased presently?"

"On ice. Downtown."

"You mean at the morgue?"

"Yes."

Mrs. Grimble finished her check boxes, then reached into her desk, pulled out some pamphlets. "These explain our various plans. Why don't you take a look?"

I gave the pamphlets a glance. Like my mother's posthumous choices, these burial options ranged from the simple and purposefully ugly to something Egyptian-style and obscenely expensive.

Mrs. Grimble recommended the client interrogatory, turning on the smarm. "Now, did you share any special memories with your uncle?"

"Let's see. He showed me my first *Playboy* magazine."

Mrs. Grimble's eyebrows drew upward as the corners of her mouth drew downward. "I see."

Inspiration struck again. "And I do have one other memory of Uncle Charles."

"Yes?" Anticipatory distaste sweetened her features.

"He won a Nathan's hot-dog eating contest."

"Really?"

"Really. He ate seventy-five of the sons of bitches." I slapped my knee. "Then he barfed like a fire hose."

Mrs. Grimble was close to the end of her professional courtesies.

"Which leads me to a problem, Mrs. Grumble. A special problem."

"The name is Grimble. What kind of special problem?"

"Mr. Glurk's size."

Mrs. Grimble's eyebrows rose again.

"Mr. Glurk weighed seven hundred and fifty-three pounds." I picked up the interment solutions pamphlet. "How wide *is* the Pharaoh's Raft?"

This was the end for Mrs. Grimble. She pushed herself to her feet.

"Would I need two plots?"

"Excuse me, Mr. Henry."

Goddammit, who were these people? Where did they come from? Why in hell had she followed Ed Grimble to Los Angeles those years ago? She should've married Gil Clayton when he'd asked. But no, Eddie Grimble had prospects. *Prospects.* Prospects for bankruptcy.

Now she encouraged the heartbroken to purchase eternity-proof bronze sepulchers on credit at ruinous terms. Life sucked. Like a dog. And she, of all people, deserved better. She had portrayed the Virgin Mother in the high school play. Brought them to tears.

Yes, she would accept moldy old Howard Lastman's invitation to dinner. Yes, she would. At the best steak house in Beverly Hills.

Did Howard still have the teeth for the job? Whatever. That would be his problem. And if he wanted a happy ending, for godsake? Presupposing the plumbing still worked. Well, she couldn't possibly *get* that drunk. He'd have to settle for crème brûlée.

Billy Ravenich was daydreaming until the knock on his door. "Key to the Highway," that beautiful eight-bar blues as done by Derek and the Dominos, faded from his mind. Clapton, Allman, Radle, Whitlock, Gordon. The masters. Perfection.

"Come in." What was it this time? Had Pablo in the back raised the dead again?

The door opened. It was that portrait of celestial pulchritude, Mrs. Grimble.

"Yes, Mrs. Grimble?"

"There's an asshole out front, Mr. Ravenich."

"What kind of asshole?"

"He's got an uncle named Glurk."

"Glurk. What kind of name is Glurk?"

"He's from Pennsylvania."

"Is there a point you're coming to, Mrs. Grimble?"

"He says his uncle weighs seven hundred pounds."

"What's this asshole's name?"

"Richard Henry."

Ravenich slapped his hand on his desk. "Thank you, Mrs. Grimble. I'll take it from here."

Ravenich strode into the lobby. And there was that righteous sphincter Dick Henry with a big smirk on his face.

*   *   *

Ravenich was glad to see me and took me back to his office. He glared at me. "Mrs. Grimble said there was an asshole out front. Seven hundred pounds. *Shit.*"

"What do you really do with a seven-hundred-pound corpse?"

"What do you think? A hoist, a chain saw, a spear, and oil for a thousand lamps."

I prefaced the subject of my visit with an inquiry into the good side of his life. "Written any tunes lately?"

He wasn't fooled. "You don't have to butter me up."

"I'm not. What are you up to?"

"Actually, I've put together a very cool unit. Set up like the Dominos. Bass, drums, keys, and me. And maybe Louie Losta on harp when he can make it. And I've written a couple of nice tunes."

"Takin' it out?"

"Tomorrow. At Nilene's in Santa Monica."

"I know where that is."

"I can expect you?"

"Quite possibly."

Ravenich snorted. "Back to my duties as a licensed funeral director. Why are you here?"

I loved Ravenich and I smiled at him.

He smiled back. "You motherfucker. How's Rojas, by the way?"

"He's fine."

"He's a good man."

"Yes, he is."

Rojas, on my recommendation, had done a little work for Ravenich. It had involved a chapel crier. The smallish, brown-haired man would show up and wail during a service. But wail to such a degree that his suffering eclipsed the pain of the truly bereaved. What the crier wanted was to be paid to go away. Ravenich had paid him a small sum but the crier had grown greedy and returned to grieve again. This time, the instant he set his mournful brown shoes in the chapel he encountered Rojas. Before he knew it he'd been led to the back room.

"What's the meaning of this?" inquired the chapel crier, irate. He knew his rights.

Rojas smashed a hard overhand right directly into the crier's chest. "Do I have your attention?" he asked.

From his position on the floor, against the wall, the man nodded, painfully, that he did.

Rojas smiled in ice. "You know what double booking is?"

The crier shook his head. It couldn't be good.

"That's where two assholes are buried in one box." Rojas picked up the crier with one arm and threw him into an empty budget coffin. "But officially," Rojas continued, "only the guy on top counts. See what I mean?"

In fact, Morton Cockley had instantaneously seen the error of his ways and was hastening to apologize but the next thing he knew was absolute blackness as Rojas slammed the lid shut. Of course, budget coffins have no interior release mechanisms.

An hour and a half later, after the longish service had concluded out front, Rojas opened up the casket. Cockley the chapel crier was a damp and changed man.

"You know what double booking is?"

"Yes."

"If you ever come here again, you're going to get double-booked for real. Understand me?"

Cockley went out the back door and was never seen again.

* * *

Ravenich grinned. "What'd Rojas say to that guy?"

"I dunno. Something about civic responsibility and respect for the dead."

"Well, whatever he said, it worked." Then Ravenich leaned forward. "So why are you here?"

"I need to file an obituary in the *Times*."

"And you want me to say the body's here."

"Are you offering?"

"What'd I tell you last time?"

"Never darken your door again." I paused. "Or words to that effect."

Ravenich nodded. "Or words to that effect."

"You're the only one who can help me."

"Bullshit. Ed Lake at Forest Lawn, Jim Harkins at Rosemont-Ross, there's—"

"I mean you're the only one who *might* help me."

"Where's the body?"

"That's the easy part."

"So where's it at?"

"There isn't one."

A sour weariness crept across Ravenich's face. "Why do I still know you? Why don't I tell you to get screwed right now?"

"Because I introduced you to Rojas. And this." I pulled an envelope from my pocket. "Here's a grand for your trouble." I put the envelope on the desk between us.

Ravenich looked askance at the packet. "You're asking me to violate a good portion of the civil code." He scratched his chin as if considering the statutes. "And you're also asking me to compromise my own moral principles."

He looked at me. I nodded. Then I reached back into my pocket and pulled out the second envelope. "Here's another fifteen hundred for your trouble."

Ravenich's gloom evaporated like a hooker's admiration after the deed was done. The envelopes disappeared into his desk.

I spread my hands. "Death is a good business."

Ravenich shrugged. "It's the family business."

CHAPTER TWENTY-EIGHT

An Obituary

I rolled down to the Canyon Country Store on Friday morning and bought the *Times.* I took a deep breath. At least one thing had gone right. I decided I'd sit outside, drink coffee, watch the traffic go by, watch the pretty Canyon girls go in and out of the market.

The *Times,* like all urban newspapers, was in steep decline, like an old friend with cancer. Robust and healthy one day, sixty pounds the next. The big, fat, heavy newspaper of my youth was gone. Now it reminded me of the miserly fish wrapper I had delivered when I'd been thirteen, the *Citizen News.*

It had been my first job. The enticement of easy money, riding my bicycle, had paled quickly. Like any job, it was work. The readership of the paper had not been inspiring, either. Composed entirely of the aged and irritable, there was nary a tip or a smile. Every day at school I basted in increasing dread of my rounds, and every day I set out a little later to accomplish them.

My tardiness dovetailed perfectly with the anxiety of my ancient clients, thirsting the whole day long for whatever excitement the *Citizen News* provided. As I would throw the paper in the general direction of the front door, I would see them, peeking through the curtains, sucking their dentures, glaring at me.

I don't remember quitting. The job just wore away. Like a bar of soap. One day it was down the drain. Which was okay by me. Even the spaz in the thick glasses who delivered the *Herald-Examiner* from a three-wheeled tip-over-proof motorbike looked down on me and the *Citizen News.*

I turned to page A-20. There was my notice.

> *Obituaries/Funeral Announcements*
> *SALT, Thomas Alva   O'Halloran Mortuary*

I added it all up. Fifteen grand for the investigation with no name. Five for the name. Fifty for the killing.

Seventy. There were worse prices for one's integrity. If I could just put the matter to rest. I called Benjamin, told him to buy the paper. He already had. He'd send Arnuldo over.

I called Ravenich, thanked him. He told me to fuck off. I asked him if he was putting the old screw to Mrs. Grimble. He hung up.

I went home, dozed off to Dylan's *Modern Times,* was dreaming of Nettie Moore when I heard a heavy knock.

Arnuldo pushed an eight-by-eleven manila envelope at me. "From Mr. B," he said, eyes narrowed and baleful.

Suddenly I felt that not only did Arnuldo dislike me, his God-given right, and none of my business, but also he bore me a very personal animosity, which was very much my business.

Why the animus?

Our first meeting, the green hat initiative, seemed almost benevolent in comparison. Nothing there.

Our next meeting. At the party, where I learned that Judy

and Lynette were the same person. Had he read my face when I dropped the drink?

If yes— Let's say *definitely* yes. He read my billboard face and intuited . . . what? That Lynette and I had history of some kind. So what?

Then he witnesses the expanding contract between me and his boss. If he sees the whole thing as a sham, is he angry on behalf of his boss? On behalf of Benjamin's money?

Or angry on behalf of himself.

And there it was. Plain as day, dark as night. Arnuldo had a thing for Lynette, platonic or otherwise. No wonder he hated me. And, by extension, hated Benjamin, boss and rival. What a happy household over on Rexford.

Arnuldo was staring at me. Looking back into his eyes, I knew he'd seen that I had figured him out. In the very second that I had. But to acknowledge the source of his rage would be to validate it.

I decided to irritate his secret injury. "You don't look good, Arnuldo. Someone squeezing your balls?"

Arnuldo, with visible effort, swallowed his feelings. "I'm fine, Henry." He could barely choke the words out. "How about you?"

"I'm fine, too. I think I might go out dancing, that's how fine I am."

"You wanna know the future, Henry?" A whisper was all he could control.

"You're a gypsy?"

"My mother was a gypsy." A pause. "One day . . . I'm going to kill you."

I shook my head. "I don't think so."

Again he swallowed. "Why won't I?"

"Why?" Here came the salt. "Because you're Mr. Benjamin's *boy* . . . and Daddy hasn't given you his permission."

That was all Arnuldo could take. He stood there, pulsating, then turned on his heel.

I heard a door slam hard. After a bit a blue Mercedes rolled soundlessly down the street.

I shut the door, tossed the envelope onto my coffee table. Thought I'd better open it.

Two sheaves of a hundred hundreds and fifty more rubber-banded. I put it back in the envelope.

I had set an enemy loose in the world. A wave of fatigue rolled over me. I refused to let it in. To anticipate pain and horror and strife is to embrace those conditions prematurely. Sufficient unto the day is the evil thereof.

With a wave of terrible longing, I wished to be in the company of my children, their little arms around my neck.

CHAPTER TWENTY-NINE

A Perfect Harmony

After dealing with some small matters, I managed to wheedle my way in at Arden. Georgette was in a good mood. I wrote her a nice check for some kitchen renovations, but she was in a good mood anyway. So I gave her an extra grand to get a new dress.

She took it calmly. "Why do you want to buy me a new dress? It won't get you anyplace."

"I've been every place, darling," I said with a wink. "Not that I'm tired of the scenery." How was that for slick? "But," I continued, "thinking as an artist, as I often do, seeing you in a new dress would make this world a better place. And I live in this world."

"Then certainly, thinking as an artist," she said, coolly returning the ball, "you've thought about shoes."

I laughed aloud. It was almost like old times. I reached into my pocket, sorted out five honeybees. I handed them over. "I insist you buy shoes."

She took the money, looked at me seriously. "Did you get rich?"

See? *See?* She loved me. Believed in me. Ha! "One day I will be, darling. But not today. But I am flush."

Randy and Martine watched this artful ballet.

"I want a new dress," said Martine, getting with the program.

"And you shall have one," I replied. I turned to my son. "Would you like a new dress, too?"

Martine shrieked with laughter. "Boys don't wear dresses! They wear pants!"

I held up a finger to disagree. "Except on certain sections of Santa Monica Boulevard."

This confused the children, bringing a frown to Georgette's face. "Dick," she warned.

I shrugged happily.

"I want a new baseball glove," said Randy. "And I would never wear a dress."

I nodded at him. "Good. I wouldn't want you to. And I'll make sure you have a new glove."

Dinner was wonderful. Basic. Wonderful. Hamburgers, green beans, and mashed potatoes with Georgette's good gravy.

We talked easily about nothing, Georgette poured me another cup of coffee, then Randy introduced a topic of significance.

"We're learning about sex at school."

I exchanged a glance with Georgette.

"Eggs and seeds and stuff," continued my son. "I know all about it. I would never do it."

"Good," I agreed. "It's messy."

"You guys did it?" Randy appraised us both.

"Did what?" inquired Martine.

I nodded. "Occasionally."

Georgette smiled a horrible smile. "We had to."

I held up two fingers. "But only twice."

"Will I have to?" Randy looked a little nervous.

"No, darling," said Georgette.

"Will I?" asked Martine. Her expression communicated the worry that, whatever it was, it probably had to be accomplished at the doctor's office in the presence of isopropyl alcohol. "Will I have to?" she asked again.

On this point Georgette and I achieved a perfect harmony. "Never," we said at the same time.

Then my phone rang.

CHAPTER THIRTY

Flowers
for a Dead Cuban

Santa Monica. As fast as I could go. And Nilene's was as far as you could go. On Ocean Avenue. Across the street the cliffs, the highway, the sea.

I thought I was through with Benjamin. But, no, this thing went on and on. Shades of Michael Corleone.

Mr. Henry? Artie Benjamin here. A pause. *I'd like to see the body.* I could imagine Arnuldo quietly nodding, smiling.

I was as close to fucked as I'd ever been. I'd been unable to reach Ravenich, but maybe it was because he was onstage with his phone off.

I left the Caddy with the valet and hurried in. The joint was dark and the band was on break but I spied Louie the harp player near the bandstand.

Louie was a very nice man and a fine, fine musician but took twenty minutes to tie his shoes, button his shirt, or say hello. Glad as I was to see him, I cut him off as he drew breath.

"Sorry, Lou. I'm in a real hurry, here. Where's Ravenich?"

Louie winked. Slowly. "Go check out back, my brother. I believe some of the peoples be smokin' that pot reefer." He talked in an exaggerated hipster patois for the pleasure of his audience.

I grasped his hand, shook it, ran for the back.

I spotted Ravenich leaning against the rear wall of the club. He was taking a hit of the mean green. I was up beside him before he knew it, startling him.

"Jesus Christ, where did you come from?"

"I need to talk to you, Billy. It's urgent."

Ravenich held up a finger. "But it'll wait. I need another poke."

Impatiently I watched him draw a connoisseur's appreciative toke. It must have been good. Cheeks puffed, he passed it in my direction. I waved him off. He shrugged, exhaled.

"Thanks for coming down, dude. What's up? Need a woman?"

"A *woman*? I would come to you for that? Why would I need a woman?"

"Because every man needs a woman. To ease his aches and pains. And I got one for you."

I looked around. "I don't have time for this, Billy."

Ravenich looked at me like I was stupid, then laid the punch line on me. "You don't have time for Elizabeth Grimble?"

Even I had to choke out a pained laugh. But Ravenich really cracked himself up. Then he started coughing. After a bit, he wiped away tears. "Now, what the fuck are you really here for?" An ancillary thought struck him. "Some hot Grimble pussy?"

Hot Grimble pussy. Now there was a piss-cutter. A piss-cutter was humor barely capable of rousing a chuckle. But Ravenich had cracked himself up again. Finally he stopped laughing. "Okay. What's up?" Another giggle escaped him.

"What's up is I need a body."

That cleared his mind a little. "A body? You think I carry bodies around in the trunk?"

"Billy, I'm dead serious. I'm in deep shit. I need a body to go along with the obituary."

"That makes you special? Every obituary needs a body. And vice versa."

"Billy, I'm in real trouble. I'm about to get fucked."

He sobered a bit. "I knew that was trouble. I knew it."

"I'll tell you when there's trouble. If my client gets to the mortuary and there's no body, then there's trouble."

The arrow of reason sailed through sensimilla space, plunked into his cerebellum. *"You're sending him to my place?"*

"Where else?"

Louie appeared on the scene. "Five minutes, my brothers."

Ravenich stared at me. "Well, you've ruined my buzz."

"I'll give you two grand to lay out someone appropriate."

"No, motherfucker, you'll give me five grand."

"Fine." Five had been my target figure.

"I take it your client thinks you whacked Mr. Salt?"

"Yes, he does."

"And how did you kill him?"

"Doesn't matter. Either blatant or sneaky. Whatever you got." I made quotation marks with my fingers. "Natural causes."

Ravenich shook his head. "This is it, by the way. Don't ask me to do another thing for you in this life."

There was only one detail left.

"Just one more thing, Billy."

"Fuck you."

"The bereaved"—I checked my watch—"will arrive, uh, soon."

"Soon? How soon?"

"Forty minutes."

"Forty minutes?" I could hear Ravenich's teeth grind. "MOTHERFUCKER," he shouted at the top of his lungs. He fished for his keys.

I had mine in my hand. "I'll be right behind you."

I ducked back into Nilene's and was halfway through the crowd when someone put a foot out and I went down hard.

I got up, caught Chuckie Gregory's fist high on my forehead, and went back down. I heard his voice, gloating. "Well, well, well. If it ain't Dick Henry." I defended my face from a shoe.

He let me up in order to knock me down with his friends watching. I faked confusion and just avoided a couple of haymakers. Then I feinted with a left and delivered a straight hard right to the solar plexus. It seemed as slow as the Foreman punch that knocked out Moorer. Down went Chuckie Gregory. I split immediately. I didn't have time to humiliate him.

I raced up Pico, made a left at Cloverfield, got on the 10 East, and floored it.

I was late to O'Halloran's. I was walking up just as Benjamin, Arnuldo, and Ravenich made their exit. I brushed my hair back, took a deep breath.

"Gentlemen."

There was a silence.

Benjamin stared coldly into my eyes. "Natural causes?"

I spread my hands. "Trade lingo."

Benjamin noticed my lumps and bruises. "You look a little lumpy."

My eye was feeling fat. "It's the humidity." Something had gone down funny, I could feel it. "Everything all right?"

"I didn't know Mr. Salt was so old, Mr. Henry."

Behind Benjamin and Arnuldo, Ravenich lifted his shoulders minutely.

What body had Ravenich laid out? I stroked my chin. When

knowledge runs out, try philosophy. "Age is point of view, I'm told."

"Perhaps. You didn't tell me he was black, either."

Ravenich lifted a single shoulder.

Old fibissedah face tried desperately to maintain his nonchalance. "You had too much class to ask, Mr. Benjamin, and he's Cuban, by the way." Put a man up on a pedestal he may stay there. So there I let it lay.

Arnuldo, behind and off to the side, looked at me and slowly drew his finger across his throat.

Benjamin's eyes bulged. "Mr. Ravich says he was a musician," he croaked through clenched teeth.

Uhhh . . . sure. Black musicians had white pussy by the truckload. That old hoodoo thing.

Ravenich's face was a mask.

I nodded to Benjamin. "Mr. Ravenich is correct. He *was* a musician."

Finally there was nothing left but bitter peace or sweet violence. Benjamin made a big swallow, nodded, walked for his Silver Cloud, Arnuldo bringing up the rear.

Ravenich and I watched them go. I turned on Ravenich. "You nearly fried my bacon. Old? *Black?*"

"It was either that or claim that Tom Salt was actually a woman. From El Salvador."

"How old was the guy you laid out?"

"Old as Benjamin."

"Shit."

"What was the guy's name?"

"Charles James. You ever heard of Charles James?"

"He *was* a musician?"

Ravenich nodded. "Played harp. Little Walter style. A Milwaukee cat."

I handed Ravenich a fifty. "Send some flowers to the service, all right?"

Ravenich examined the face of Ulysses S. Grant. "Uh, fifty bucks buys budget flowers."

I'd had all I could take. "For chrissakes, Billy, just send the man some flowers."

CHAPTER THIRTY-ONE

Lips and Tongue

Arnuldo guided the Silver Cloud onto the 10 and across town at eighty-five smooth miles an hour. The dead black man he had just seen had nothing to do with anything. And asshole Dick Henry was a fraud. Was he covering up for Judy? Or involved with Judy? Didn't matter. If they crossed paths and opportunity were present, the man's days were numbered.

He eyed Mr. Benjamin in the rearview mirror. The man was suffering.

So, suffer. *Magdusa.*

Arnuldo remembered the night of his first real conversation with Mrs. Benjamin. All their previous interactions had been incidental and formal. There was no conceivable benefit in talking to Mr. B's woman and he hadn't.

They met in the kitchen. All other staff being out, and Mr. Benjamin on business in San Francisco, she had asked him to make her a sandwich.

He made her a BLT with thin-sliced avocado by way of his razor-sharp butterfly knife and they'd gotten to talking and he found himself telling his tale.

He talked of Tondo and his mother. Of Olongapo City,

134

Delia, Mr. Dinkins, of the trip to paradise. Of the phone call he had received four years later. That Delia had died in flames in an accident with a wrong-way driver on the freeway.

How he had loved Delia! With a fervency and quality he could never bring to the light of day. His last connection with his homeland. And though she had not loved him, had not recognized the burning orb in his chest, she was kind and that was something.

Then, within months of her passing, Dinkins had perished at sea. He had fallen over the side on the ship's passage from Long Beach to Pearl Harbor. The USS *St. Louis,* LKA 116. An amphibious cargo transport. The death was attributed to misadventure at sea. But Arnuldo knew better. Mr. Dinkins had died of a broken heart. The sea was merely his resting place.

The deaths of Delia and Mr. Dinkins had severed all emotional connection, had set him free, free from hope, free from human obligation. He had embraced the void.

As he recounted their deaths, tears came to her eyes and her hand accidentally touched his.

Except there are no such accidents.

With infinite mutual subtlety the brush became a hold. While his hands were in hers, and their eyes upon each other, something happened. Slowly, ever so slowly, she leaned across the table and kissed him lightly, so lightly, on the lips. The second kiss was deeper and full of passion.

There was no question in his mind that he was doing the wrong thing, that he was giving license to huge trouble. But he was Arnuldo, from Tondo, raised from ruin, destined for solitude, his fate that he would scatter to the wind the little he would gather together.

The knock he had both anticipated and feared came at half

past eleven. He was not close to sleep. Though that's what he pretended when he opened his door and she walked right in.

Over the course of the evening they made love in every possible fashion. He even went down between her legs and pleasured her with his lips and tongue. Which he had never done before. A practice he had crudely abhorred in the company of his rough friends from National City. Apparently he had been good at it.

From that day forth, he had been her willing slave. And from that day, like a cancer growing from a single malignant cell, he had begun to hate Mr. Benjamin.

The Silver Cloud exited the 10 at La Cienega and proceeded north.

"Arnuldo."

"Yes, boss?"

"Take Sunset, swing by Liquor Locker."

"Yes, boss."

CHAPTER THIRTY-TWO

Some Rest
for the Wicked

I rolled out of O'Halloran's and didn't want to drive on the freeway so I drove home on surface streets, finally reached my place. To the dregs of my soul I yearned for the temporary absolution of sleep. As I turned the key, I heard a voice.

"Hi, Dick."

It was Lynette.

That night, when I thought all had been squandered, we got back to heaven's groove. We flowed together; no words were necessary. Perhaps we had no place else to go. We made love slowly and my weariness fell away and the universe was a benevolent place. We lay in the dark and I wanted nothing, wanted for nothing. There was no past, there was no future. Just this moment of absolute peace. The tiniest breeze eddied in from the garden, and I could feel its soundless tide, in and out, over my face. The crickets did their work, I had done mine, and everything was as all right as it was ever going to get.

CHAPTER THIRTY-THREE

Patricia's Dream

It wasn't much of a dream, but she had worked on it. Now, again, little Patricia Anne Nagle, age eleven, took the stage at St. Cecelia Parish Hall. As her hands descended softly to the keys, a sense of happy confidence filled her up, from tiptoes to tip-top. She had practiced "Für Elise" countless times. It was almost as if she'd written it herself.

The melody spun out across the hall, and the hearts of all who heard it moved with it; they were comforted and transported to a place beyond woe and confusion. The liquid, self-evident mathematics of melody and harmony took the several hundred individual listeners and recast them as one entity. And that one entity held its breath and prepared itself for the sweet agony of finale.

Patricia Anne sounded the final chord and then, at exactly the right moment, removed her hands from the keys.

Into that perfect blessed silence fell the approbation of the crowd. It crashed into the vacuum, then outward against the walls, reverberating, everyone on their feet, applauding, cheering, whistling, yelling. And in the front row was a beautiful lady, on her feet, proudest of them all. The beautiful lady had hazel eyes, lambent orbs of kindness and love, and these wonderful eyes were focused entirely on Patricia Anne.

The beautiful lady was her mother, and the supreme happiness of that single moment suffused Patricia Anne's entire being, dissolved it in joy, rendered it incapable of shame, of dirt, of disappointment.

Sometimes she ran back the dream again and again, took the stage one more time in the fragile hush of expectation. This time, she pushed herself up, looked down on Dick Henry, then walked to the kitchen to get herself a drink of water.

The water ran over her fingers. In actuality, her memories of her mother were few, flashes here and there. Then there were the numerous bastard conflated fictions, true memories mixed up with the recollections of others telling her their versions of what they thought she must have experienced.

Her father had called her into the bedroom that evening. She was six years old. That day was a blur; she had been carrying on and on about something, whatever it was, refusing to make peace with it.

"I'll give you something to cry about, Patricia," said her father, hands heavy on her shoulders. "Mama's in heaven."

Richard Nagle looked down on his daughter. His life had fallen completely apart at eleven-sixteen that morning. How would he tell Patricia? How would he usher in the very worst day of her little life? She stared up at him. "Mama's gone to heaven," he repeated slowly. He had a feeling she had not understood the meaning of his words.

"When is she getting back?" asked Patricia Anne.

Now the water was cold. She filled a glass and drank it off. Los Angeles water was some of the best in the entire country.

Yet millions of the city's citizens drank bottled water in a mass billion-dollar delusion that it was better. Proof of tap water's relative purity didn't sway them. Barnum had been exactly right. Suckers were born every day.

And it didn't stop there. The sickening, frightening, cold-comedic fraud of this loveless world. Which no one wanted to acknowledge.

Every single face the face of a liar. Every liar claiming truth. There was no merit, there was connection. There was no right way, there were ways. The front way meant you had friends, the back way meant you used money, and the side way meant you used whatever you had. No one was straight, nothing was true, everyone was crooked, everyone was on the take, everything was for sale. But at the highest level of the game, where a man was manicured, pedicured, shampooed, shaved, and blow-jobbed, you never, never, never admitted it was a game. You played with a straight face and made sure your cuff links were polished.

She went back into the bedroom and looked down on Dick Henry. His body was still good and his face was lined but you could see the kid in it. He'd probably played third base or something. The hot corner, that's what they called it. Hey, batta, batta.

He was still a kid. Hadn't seen it was all false, all a game, all a deception, all a ruin.

She climbed into bed and lay beside him, smelled his scent, timed his respiration, joined it. Was it possible, was it faintly, minutely, microscopically possible that the game was not a game? That it was real? That love was not an angle?

She moved her forehead against his shoulder, put her hand over his forearm.

Then she closed her eyes.

CHAPTER THIRTY-FOUR

Tom Salt Is Dead

Artie Benjamin looked into his backyard and was pleased. Water arced rhythmically over the lawn, deconstructed into diamond shards of beauty by the late morning sun. Roy G. Biv. Red, orange, yellow, green, blue, indigo, violet. But you don't want to drink it.

And where was Judy last night? Well, fuck her. He had some news for her.

How had he allowed himself to marry her? He hated looking back but couldn't help it. His courtship—*courtship*—had been a movie. A willing suspension of disbelief. Except he'd been paying for popcorn at lobster prices. And when time enough had passed so that he could look at the truth and the third woman he'd made his wife, there he was, sitting in a pile of shit. Why? Because Arthur Benjamin, as his father had claimed a thousand times, was as stupid as the day was long.

Even his mother thought he was stupid. Well, eff all of them. His mother, his father, Judy, his uncles and the rest. Arthur Andrew Benjamin had made $50 million of his own.

Judy had crawled in at five. Slept behind her locked door. Now he heard feet on the stairs. The big clock in the living room bonged out eleven.

And here she was. In that long green silk bathrobe he'd purchased at a great price. Cantonese silk. But how was he to really know? Maybe it was Orlon from Santee Alley.

She was smoking a cigarette and holding the newspaper. Yet even knowing all that he knew, her sheer beauty, her sheer freakish beauty had its effect on him. If only she loved him.

Judy, without a word in his direction, sat down at the other end of the very long kitchen table. She brushed a tress of dark hair from her face. Agnalcia brought her breakfast in; he watched Judy ignore her utterly.

"Coffee," said Judy to Agnalcia's back.

Not an eye toward him. Toward the man who provided everything. So be it. If she wasn't talking, neither was he. He had his pride and silence was the price.

But, after a while, he couldn't hold out. "Good morning, dear," he sang, in deep falsehood.

Judy did not look up. She took a drag on her cigarette. Agnalcia delivered her coffee.

"Cream," said Judy to Agnalcia's back.

"I didn't hear you come in last night, darling."

Not the slightest reaction from Judy. With her latest Barneys bill coming in at $6,500. With another couple of grand at Kenneth Cole. Judy had brought forth in him feelings he had thought mutually incompatible. He wanted to bash her face in and at the same time he felt at the edge of tears, loving her, loving her.

"We've come a long way since our wedding day, haven't we, darling?"

"Screw you, Artie." She flicked her cigarette into her eggs. She was sick of being reminded how much he had done for her. The depths of her ingratitude.

He suppressed his anger. "By any chance, have you read the obituaries this week?"

She didn't look up. "Are you dead yet?"

"That's funny. My only conclusion is that you didn't see the news."

Finally she looked up at him. "What news?"

"What news?" he mimicked. She hated that.

She picked up her fork and threw it toward the working end of the kitchen. "More coffee."

Then she looked at him. "What possible news might there be that would be both important to you *and* important to me?"

"Maybe you haven't heard, darling. Tom Salt is dead."

If he hadn't known better, he would have thought she appeared honestly puzzled. "Who's Tom Salt?"

The bile in his stomach rose in sour glee. "Tom Salt is one dead son of a bitch. That's all you need to know."

She continued feigning ignorance. "How'd he die?"

Benjamin made quote marks in the air. "Natural causes."

Artie Benjamin was honestly stupid but this Tom Salt crap had her honestly confused. She looked at her husband. *Husband.* "Is there something I'm not getting? Who's Tom Salt? Do you have some of his CDs or something?"

Aha. Ravich had been right. Salt *was* a musician. Well, the black-assed fucker had played his last low-down blues.

Benjamin leaned back, folded his arms across his chest, shook his head. "You know, you're really something, you know that? You're a much better actress than I thought." She was still looking at him blankly. "But it doesn't change the truth."

She gave up. He was talking in riddles. "Look, I'm not clairvoyant. *What in hell* are you talking about?" She stabbed out her cigarette in the fruit cup.

Benjamin felt a cold calm. A man did what he had to do. "I'll repeat the news, bitch. Tom Salt is dead. And it's no accident."

Judy got to her feet, slung the plate down the counter and off the table, where it shattered on the Italian marble in an eggy mess. "Well, Artie, what can I say? Fuck the both of you."

CHAPTER THIRTY-FIVE

Incursion

Hodgekiss was a doleful soul with a small office on South La Cienega above the 10 freeway. He was a forensic document examiner which meant he hated all others of his kind. They were all blind, corrupt incompetents worming their way through the soft loam of an imprecise science in service of the legal system. Luckily for the public, he, Carl F. Hodgekiss, was available for general consultation.

I had not found Hodgekiss through his reputation. He was a poker buddy of Myron Ealing. He was a reliable loser who brought Costco platters.

Hodgekiss studied the Francie–Tillman letters and the Philippine mission address of Linscomb's.

"So, what do you think?" I had told him of Linscomb's ambidexterity.

"Well, Mr. Henry, I would say it's a strong possibility. An eighty percenter. You can't rule him out."

Which is as good as you get with handwriting analysis. I had done a little reading on the JonBenét Ramsey case. Fifty experts swore Patricia Ramsey, her mother, had written the ransom note. Forty-nine experts, equally adamant, called the fifty misguided fools.

It came down to this. If you didn't actually see someone write the document in question, there would always be questions about its authorship.

But Linscomb *could* have written it.

I called in my Irregulars from assignment in the field. That night, Bobby and Lenny stopped by with a week's information about Linscomb.

Linscomb lived quietly. No visitors. Liked Thai food. Shopped at Smart & Final. Purchased pricey tequila at Liquor Locker. Exercised in Runyon Canyon, walking up to Mulholland and back.

Wednesday at lunch, he procured an eighth ounce of medical marijuana from Dill's on Santa Monica in West Hollywood. He did this every Wednesday. That Thursday night, at 10:47, he quietly exited his apartment, started up his late-model white Honda Civic, negotiated the twists and turns of Laurel Canyon Boulevard into the valley. There he drove north and eastward, his destination the Barracks, a bathhouse in NoHo right behind Circus Liquor. At 2:17 A.M. he arrived back at church property. At 9:00 A.M. he left his apartment and walked the fifty steps to the rectory, resuming his duties for Christ.

All this information proved nothing; neither did it exclude him from suspicion.

"He's a butt pirate, Dick," said Bobby, elbowing Lenny.

"A butt pirate for Christ," summed Lenny, in paroxysms.

"Live and let live," I counseled, "more pussy for the rest of us." I paid them and they left.

Once these boys had lived a little longer, they might appreciate the concept of whatever-gets-you-through-the-night. Life was a bitch, from everyone you loved you'd be separated, and then you died. So, whatever distractions you found, as long as they didn't hurt children, they were okay with me.

But you paid for those distractions. Like I had paid. On those long, empty nights when I had sought the additional comforts of floozies, I had surrendered the company of Georgette.

Supposedly, there was a place where you could have your cake and eat it, too. Europe. But that was a long way from Los Angeles, the most modern city in the world, stuffed, from ocean shore to mountaintop, with sanctimonious charlatans. And so, from Aimee Semple McPherson in the 1920s to contemporary TV evangelists smoking meth and screwing Boy Scouts, human nature broke out, relentlessly, as soon as the sun went down.

It brought me a certain pleasure to think that the next tawdry headline event had already taken place. Anxious parties were scurrying this minute to cover it up.

But the cover-up won't work and the ugly boil will burst and the talking heads will soon be frothing with grateful indignation, declaiming the death of all things decent.

Deep down I'm skeptical of Europe, too. Because it's populated by human beings and human beings everywhere are jealous, spiteful, ungrateful, and envious. Also loving and lovely and caring and generous.

It's all a mess. Which is why they need the Shortcut Man every so often. To sort things out.

On Saturday night at midnight, Lenny and Bobby called from the vicinity of Circus Liquor. Linscomb had just checked in to the Barracks.

Perfect. I rolled down from Laurel Canyon, parked on Vista above Hollywood. It wasn't his vices I objected to. It was the fact that vices cost money, that they were possibly untenable on a church salary. I entered his apartment with no trouble, started looking around.

Linscomb was neat as a pin, a place for everything. And, no doubt, his mind was equally compartmentalized. That would be the way he would excuse certain behaviors.

In his antique rolltop desk, in one of the pigeonhole drawers, I found some bindled white powder and some fragrant green. Then, neatly stowed in one of the six narrow vertical slots, reminiscent of the fabled purloined letter, I found what I was looking for. A manila envelope labeled "The Ballad of Franklin Tillman."

Not only did I find copies of the letters I had read at the Farmers Market but I also found a brief outline for a piece of fiction about a growing relationship between a lonely old man and the woman he corresponds with—except the woman is really a lonely young man in disguise. There was some question as to its final form. A play? A screenplay? A book? And the ending had not been entirely worked out. Research was in progress. But it would be poignant and emotional.

I wiped away a tear. Little did the author know that right this moment, as he chambered a fat cock in NoHo, I, Dick Henry, the Shortcut Man, the unlikeliest of authors, had fashioned the ending for him.

CHAPTER THIRTY-SIX

Jerry Plays His Cards

Jerry Shunk looked at himself in the mirror. Sheila, of the big knockers, had been right. Salon Seven Seven had been the place to go. What had that black girl called this hair color? Montana something . . . that was it, Montana Smoke.

Yes, he looked fifty-five. But a cool fifty-five. A fighting fifty-five. Through the evidence of time, which lent some character, others age, he still could make out the young man with ideals. Of course, ideals had been thrown in the fire a long time ago. Ideals were like the clothes he'd worn at Cornell, now way too small and seriously out of fashion. Corduroys and wide belts and suede boots, thinking that one man could change the world.

One man *could* make a difference, of course, but a lot of ducks had to be in a row at the exact moment your hand found the gun, aimed, and fired. The synchrony of those phenomena was a statistical nightmare. And then you had to hit something. There was one man who could reliably make a difference. Dad. Your dad. Your *rich* dad. Shunk's father was a pharmacist. Pharmacists didn't make shit.

Mr. Rutledge was the first man whose will Shunk had rewritten posthumously. Rutledge had no living relatives, all his assets would have gone to the government. A stupid, criminal waste. The government paid thousands of dollars for toilet seats, hundreds for a nail.

So what had he done? In realistic parlance, he had redistributed capital. As it trickled down. Where had it gone? To the public. Employing others, providing a modicum of pleasure for himself as it passed through his fingers. Like the story of the dying Irishman asking his dearest friend to pour a bottle of whiskey over his grave. The dear friend agreed but asked if he might strain it through his kidneys first.

Shunk had married twice and divorced twice, always disappointed with the women behind the makeup. But not as disappointed as they were with him. Bitches. Blind to the realities of life. Blind to the fact that a man had to provide in a world where conscience was a hindrance. So off they went, Judith and Devorah, reclaiming their innocence and freedom—except with alimony sufficient to maintain a reasonable quality of life.

He had specialized in family law, then geriatric family law. Every so often, though not enough to establish pattern or arouse suspicion, a grateful oldster, unencumbered by grasping relatives, would leave him everything.

And very, very, very rarely, of which the überancient Mrs. Cutler at Fairfax Convalescent might be the best example, he would speed them gently on their way, cutting short their pointless misery. That time with a Chinese duck-down pillow.

He spritzed on some Armani cologne. Seventy-five dollars for a hundred milliliters. Devorah had called him an Aqua Velva man. Fuck her.

Shunk had known Artie Benjamin since college. Seen him through a couple of divorces and half a dozen abortions. Then his sudden success in porn. *Buffalo Bill in Hollywood.* And some asshole called it art.

Which led to Benjamin's third marriage, to that Vegas pole dancer. Judy had called Shunk up a couple of years after the honeymoon and told him to buy her some lunch. He did as ordered. She'd probably scratched Artie's Rolls.

There was a nice little bistro on Hillhurst near Franklin. After twenty minutes of her company, he hated Benjamin. Because he envied him so completely. Judy's mouth would've shamed a sailor, but she was rescued by an intoxicating insouciance. He had never desired anything quite as much as this woman.

When lunch was over she had him drive up into Griffith Park. They sparked up a joint and watched the merry-go-round. Just a few kids and their dark nannies. But then she surprised him.

She started unbuttoning her blouse. It took a while because her blouse seemed to have eighty-five buttons. Then she opened it up and showed him her rack. She didn't need a bra and wasn't wearing one. Those little brown, upturned nipples were the most incendiary things he'd ever seen. She thumbed a nipple, and it stiffened as he watched.

"Suck my titties," said Judy, offering them.

Oh, good Lord, he had.

Then she reached between his legs and, unbelievably, set him free. Looking into his eyes, she licked her lips, then leaned down and placed her luscious mouth over his cock.

Sixty timeless seconds later he experienced the most intense orgasm of his life. When he opened his eyes he was surprised he still had a spine.

She was looking at him, grinning. "Hasn't anyone ever sucked your cock before, Jerry?"

No. Not even. Not like that. "What do you want?" he whispered, shuddering to breathe.

She laughed. "I need your help."

"With what?"

"With Artie's will."

"It sounds like you have a plan already."

"I do."

He smiled at himself in the mirror. Bloodthirsty bitch. And not once since that sixty seconds in heaven had that bitch laid even a finger on him.

Well, today might be the day. He had information that would change her life. He swallowed a Cialis.

This time they met for lunch downtown at Cafe Merlot. She was late, but late was the province of beautiful women. Then she arrived. He saw heads turn, and he read their jealous little minds.

Look at her! Good God! What a woman! Look at the rack on that girl! And who's that guy with her? Why, I believe that's Jerry Shunk! It can't be Jerry Shunk. What happened to Jerry Shunk? It *is* Jerry Shunk! What's Jerry Shunk doing with a girl like that? Shunk must have game! Shunk's got game!

He rose to embrace her and felt her chest crush against his own. He pulled out her chair, and she sat.

She ordered expensive appetizers and picked. Which rankled his natural frugality, but, Jesus, she was so unbelievably gorgeous.

And that goddam Cialis was kicking in early. It was the wrong time for a raging five-hour hard-on. Well, it was early. He wouldn't be able to get up without two copies of the *L.A. Times.* But he wouldn't call his physician, either. He'd fuck Judy, half a dozen waitresses, then an eggplant or two. Christ, he had a rocket in his pocket. And he'd learned something new. You couldn't talk yourself into a hard-on when you needed one, and the inverse, you couldn't talk yourself out of one if it wasn't the time. If that wasn't life in a nutshell, nothing was. The tragedy of life.

"You all right, Jerry?" she asked. Shitbird in his blue hair was working something out in his head.

"Fine, darling." Her rack sucked his eyes in. If he were any closer his eyes would be crossed. He had to focus over her shoulder. Where that sparrow was playing with . . . a fucking condom! The sparrow was playing with a used condom in the ficus tree. Jesus Christ. Filthy birds. They'd pick up anything.

Judy looked cross. She pushed her appetizers away. "Jerry. Tell me what was so important that we had to come here."

Bitch. Beautiful bitch.

Jerry looked deep into Judy's green eyes and lied, unspooling the first careful strands of the narrative he had created. "I had a call from Artie. He wants to start proceedings."

"That's bad, right?"

"That's bad."

"When does that prenup stuff turn real?"

"When it's filed with the court. And you'll get your two hundred fifty thousand." A pittance. "But remember." This was the sweet part. "A prenup only kicks in when you're *getting* divorced. If he should have an accident while the marriage is extant . . ."

And there it lay.

The calm, chill waters of the temptatious Rubicon. The clatter of silverware and raucous bray of conversation receded into nothingness. After a small eternity, she spoke. "How long do we have?"

We. Jerry looked into her perfect face. Bloodthirsty, greedy bitch. How perfectly convenient. And he could have her, too, if he played his cards right. "An accident after the filing won't look good."

He shrugged. But, yes. If Artie should have an accident while the marriage was extant . . . only the will would remain. Only the will. And he had carefully, subtly rewritten the will.

Judy reached for his hands. She was crying. They should have invented tear-proof mascara by now. Except tears were a weapon. You don't give away weapons.

She dabbed at her eyes with the white linen napkin. "Sometimes I'm so afraid, Jerry."

The way she enunciated his name was like a tongue on the tip of his cock. "Don't worry, doll. It's taken care of."

Yes, Judy, dear, Artie's will is all taken care of. No matter who came and went, the winner would be Jerry Shunk. Sidebet Jerry Shunk. Never too greedy, never too needy, always a winner.

"We'll share everything, won't we, Jerry?"

"Yes, doll. We will." If you're not convicted of murder.

CHAPTER THIRTY-SEVEN

A Star
in His Own Movie

This time I parked on Sierra Bonita. Lenny had called. Linscomb was back at the Barracks.

At two-fifteen I heard his feet on the stairs, then the key in the door. He stepped into the quiet darkness, flipped on the entry light, a small Tiffany lamp with a candlestand base. Into the candlestand he dropped his keys. He engaged the chain lock. A tired sigh escaped him. He'd taken three steps toward the kitchen when he realized someone was sitting at the round oak table in the shadows.

"Jesus Christ!" he gasped.

"Sit down, Mr. Linscomb."

He stood stock-still, frozen between fight and flight.

"Don't run, Mr. Linscomb. Because I'll catch you. Have a seat."

Flight, an instantaneous reaction, had been eschewed by nonaction. Maybe he would come at me.

No, he would not come at me. Fright had him paralyzed.

"I'm—I'm going to let you walk out of here," said Linscomb. "Like this never happened."

155

I just stared at him.

"I'm letting you walk out of here," he amended. Moving from future to present. "If you go right now."

I looked at him. "Why don't you have a seat and we'll talk. And then I'll decide what I want to do. 'Cause maybe I want to fuck you up."

His hands were shaking.

He came forward, pulled out a chair across the table from me, sat slowly. "Do I know you?" He studied me. "I *do* know you."

"Reverend Jenkins said you were a writer."

"I *do* know you. I can find out your name. Your soul was in peril."

"Yes. And now your ass is in peril. My name is Dick Henry."

Linscomb spread his hands. "Look, man. I don't understand where our lives intersect. I think you must have some bad information."

"The point of intersection is Franklin Tillman."

This was a hard left to the gut. He stopped breathing for a second. "I don't know what you're talking about and—"

"Don't insult me with bullshit, *Francie.* You've been writing to Tillman, wheedling away his money. That's why I'm here. I represent Mr. Tillman's interest. I'm not the police, and I don't give a shit about your rights."

The stone-cold, tactile silence of 2:30 A.M. filled the room.

I slid the sheaf of letters over in front of him. "So tell me, fuckstick. What made you think you could screw Franklin Tillman and get away with it?"

He licked his lips, swallowed. Breathed. Whispered. "I don't know."

"I do. You think you're smarter than everyone else and don't have to play by the rules."

Linscomb's head sank into his hands.

"If you start sobbing, I'm going to beat the shit out of you."

Linscomb pulled himself back from the brink, his eyes full.

"You got any of his money left?"

"Uh, I, uh—"

"Don't say *What money?* How much of his fourteen grand do you have left?"

"Uh . . . nothing. A few hundred. I used it as I went along."

"How are you going to make it up to him?"

Another silence. Far away, down on Sunset probably, a siren started to whine.

"How are you going to make it up to him, fuckstick?"

A whisper. "I don't know. What do I *do?*"

"First we put an end to this."

"Okay. It's over."

"Not quite that easy. You're going to write one more letter."

"Okay."

"From Francie's brother. He's going to write to Franklin and explain how she died."

"Died?"

"With Franklin's name on her lips."

For the next five minutes that's what we did. As he wrote, he told me that writing is mostly rewriting and was segueing into a scholarly disquisition but I wasn't having it. "Shut the fuck up and write." Finally the letter was complete.

"When do you deliver Franklin's letters?"

"When the packet comes from Manila."

"When will that happen?"

"Next Tuesday, thereabouts."

"How does he get his letters?"

"I call him. He comes by."

"Fine. You'll make sure he gets this letter, and then you'll resign your position as of that day and you'll say your good-byes on Sunday."

"That's not much notice. That's not going to sit well with Reverend Jenkins."

"Maybe I should talk to the reverend."

He sat there for a second. "No."

How do you deal with a spider in church? You step on it.

But Linscomb was feeling confessional. "You know I never meant this to go where it did. It just happened."

"Nothing just happens. Show me the picture that started all this."

He looked at me, surprised. "How did you know?"

"Just show me the goddam picture."

"Okay." He rose, went to his desk, opened a drawer, returned with a photograph, eight by ten, handed it to me.

Seven people waved from the front door of a three-story building in the sun. A cross, slightly askew, hung over the door.

"Which one is Francie?"

He pointed at a cheerful looking Filipina, late forties.

Part of me smiled. *All right,* Franklin. Going after that young stuff.

There was a formula for the proper age difference between men and women. Though I was unsure where it came from, I had no doubt of its masculine origin.

Half a man's age plus seven.

Which meant Lynette was perfect for me. And for Franklin, let's see, uh, seventy-eight, thirty-nine, uh, forty-six. Francie could have been forty-six. *All right,* Franklin. "What's her real name?"

"I'm not sure. I think it's Josie." He paused. "I never did anything like this before."

Bullshit.

"You know, in one way he owes me."

Disgust is ameliorated by exposure. Over the time I'd been in his company I'd started to feel a little sorry for him. But Linscomb's last pronouncement reversed the process. I felt a tingle in my fist. "In one way he *owes* you?"

"Sure he does. I made him the star in his own movie. Franklin Tillman, *Adventure in Manila.* I've given the man his last thrill."

I thought of Tillman a little differently. Korean War vet, couple of Purple Hearts. A family man, a mechanical engineer at Aerojet, an individual with a conscience who suffered the slings and arrows of being a good man in a shitty world. And then, in *church,* in his final years, he runs into Michael Linscomb.

It was karma time.

I struck like a serpent, pinned the guy's right wrist to the table with my left hand. Then, with my right, I bent his thumb all the way back to his wrist. He could have been double-jointed, but he wasn't. There was a sharp, bright-sounding crack accompanied by a scream.

He snatched his hand back, high in the air. His thumb depended oddly, and it seemed he couldn't believe what he was seeing. "My thumb. *My thumb.* It's *broken.* You broke my thumb."

"Yes, I did. But don't worry. My friend Dr. Clarke would call this a simple diaphyseal fracture. Anyway, you're ambidextrous; you can write with your other hand."

I snapped my fingers. "And maybe you can put this in a movie, too. The sequel to *Adventure in Manila.* You can call it *Tillman's Revenge.*"

I got up, looked down at him. "If you're not out of here on

Sunday, fuckstick, things will go poorly for you. Maybe you'll be one of those guys who learns to write with his feet."

I walked out before I skinned him alive.

Reverend Jenkins had been briefly awakened that night by what he thought may have been a scream. But it couldn't have been. Not in this neighborhood. He turned back over. He needed all the sleep he could get. Tomorrow morning, like every morning, he would celebrate five-thirty Mass.

CHAPTER THIRTY-EIGHT

Breaking Up
Is Hard to Do

I'd imagined it would have gone like this. Because it had to be done, no way around it.

It would be late, maybe one in the morning. There'd be a knock. A knock I'd recognize as hers. I'd open up and there she'd be, tragically beautiful, tragically flawed. With that smile on her face. She'd walk right in like she owned the place. "What's up, Dick Henry?"

I'd have to smile but that smile would have shadows and she'd pick that up.

What's wrong?

Nothing's wrong.

Something's wrong.

And then, unlike most real instances in my life, I would just tell the woman the truth.

Look. You know it and I know it. It's just not working. Between us. We should close the book on this one.

Her expression would ratify the truth of my words.

Break up?

I think so. *Shit.* I'd have to do better than *I think so.*

161

Break up?

Yes.

She'd flop down on the couch, toss her purse on the coffee table, lean back, shut her eyes.

She'd open her eyes, they'd be moist. You're right, you're right, she'd say.

It's better this way.

I know it is.

Then would come statements of mutual respect and admiration. Then further statements of ameliorative fallacy.

Maybe I'll see you around.

Yeah. You never know.

In a perfect world, she would pick up her stuff, walk toward the door. I'd get there first, open it. We'd both step out onto the porch. Since this was my fantasy, I let a misty rain fall softly, hissing into the foliage.

She'd turn and look at me. Except for her green eyes, this would be a Willie Nelson "Blue Eyes Crying in the Rain" moment.

Then we'd kiss. A deep, soulful kiss, unhurried and salutary. Carrying memories and echoes of faded love, offering hints and glints of vistas never to be seen.

We'd separate, look into each other's eyes.

Good-bye, Dick.

Good-bye, What's-Your-Name.

Of course, I wouldn't say that.

Good-bye, Lynette.

She would turn, descend the three steps from the porch to the walkway, and walk to the gate. Never looking back, she'd open the gate, step through, let it fall shut behind her.

I would never see her again.

Our breakup would preface my meteoric rise to success and

renown. Mutual friends would sadly describe her, bereft and alone, doggedly compiling a scrapbook of my accomplishments.

Eventually she would die in Paris. I mean, expire . . . expire in Paris.

Her knock came at two-fifteen. I had just finished a Preston Sturges DVD, my favorite among them, *Unfaithfully Yours.* His one Fox picture. Rex Harrison, Linda Darnell, Rudy Vallee. And the Sturges gang with Al Bridge.

I opened up and she breezed right in, a half-smoked joint dead between her fingers. Unfaithfully mine. "What's up, Dick Henry?"

I smiled. We kissed lightly. She tossed her purse onto the coffee table. Then she tipped her head, looked at me.

"What's wrong?"

"Nothing's wrong."

"Something's wrong."

Breaking up in real life is much harder than in the rehearsal. You are assailed by doubts about your own feelings, you are filled with sudden sympathy for the partner about to be sundered, sudden fears concerning consequence. What if this is the last straw between her and suicide? Between suicide and blowing your fucking head off with the small-caliber pistol you never knew she carried in her purse? Because you never know what's in a woman's purse.

"Look," I began, "you and I know this is not working."

"What's not working?"

"You know what's not working. Maybe we should close the book on this one."

"What book?"

"You know what I'm talking about."

"You want to break up with me?"

"Yes."

"Well, fuck you, Dick."

And then she leapt into my arms, grabbed me by the head, and kissed me deep and long. My intellect persevered for a few seconds then folded its tent, disappeared. I carried her straight to the bedroom, and we set right in.

Every act of love is an act of communication. Most times not profound, simply serving to remind partners that something very personal, something beyond words does exist. It beats arguing. We made love slowly and deeply, almost sadly, then it was finished.

We lay there in the half-light and the quiet, breathing. A couple of Japanese motorcycles snarled up the canyon. She turned over, touched my arm. "It's over, isn't it, Dick?"

"Yeah."

The word rolled right out, like a marble from a jar, a single syllable, irretrievable, irrevocable. Shocking. What part of me had answered that question?

I made some coffee, we sat in the kitchen. Words were a physical effort.

She made a sound that resembled a laugh. "Well, you did all right on this one, Dick."

"What are you talking about? I did all right how?"

"Money-wise."

"Money-wise?"

Ojai entered and formed in her mind. That clean, square Craftsman house and the children she would never have and the impossibility, futility, stupidity, insanity, inanity, foolishness, and laughability of everything. Had she really thought she loved this man? This two-bit player? This scratch hitter? This rambler? This wanderer? This refugee? This foot soldier?

Had she allowed herself to believe in something other than the real? Other than the present? Other than the factual? The manifest? The tactile? The smelly? That which will rot? Had she invested in that hilarious fiction, love? When she knew better? *Knew better?* Love was nothing but a stupid fantasy, a wish, a prayer, a petition into a mirror.

Well, she had come back to her senses. The target was Artie. "Yeah, you did all right, Dick." She rubbed thumb and forefinger. "Creating Tom Salt. Killing Tom Salt. Fucking brilliant. Accepting Artie's money for killing a person who didn't exist. Yeah, you did all right."

"How did you know about Tom Salt?"

"And your fifty grand? It doesn't matter how I know."

"Oh, yes it does."

"Then I'll let you figure it out." She got to her feet, picked up her purse, walked out of the kitchen, through the little hallway toward the front door. "Good-bye, Dick."

She walked outside. Toward the gate.

"Where're you going?"

She paused, looked over her shoulder at me. "Back. Back to the real world."

Pearly King kept running through my head. Pearly King and the Temple Thieves. Pearly, E.G. Houston, Byrd Sancious, Osvado Oquendo. The tune was called "Ghost of a Ghost."

> *I fell asleep*
> *You were in my head*
> *Woke up soakin' wet*
> *You were in my bed*
> *Ghost of a ghost of a ghost*
> *But you won't fade away*

Rain of the rain of the rain come down every day
A car rolls by in the street
Your perfume it lingers so sweet
I don't have the will to pretend
Baby yes I'm drinkin' again

But Lynette had tipped her hand. And there it was, the classic case of the Inside Man. When she'd mentioned Artie's fifty grand, all the relationships solidified.

She shouldn't have known that figure. Artie wouldn't have told her that figure, would he? And who else would know . . . except Arnuldo. Love struck Arnuldo.

Lynette was too smart for her own good. She was in the center of the circle, and around her danced the marionettes, to be drawn close as necessary. Artie, Arnuldo, Jerry Shunk.

And Dick Henry.

But Dick Henry didn't care anymore.

CHAPTER THIRTY-NINE

The Inside Man

Well after midnight the clouds broke, releasing the benefi-
cence of a distant god to his multitudes in the canyons, the
arroyos, and the flats. My back window was open, and I lis-
tened to it come down.

I couldn't sleep.

Then, through the pounding of the rain, I became aware of
another sound. Someone at the door.

Through the side window I saw it was Arnuldo. He was
holding another eight-by-eleven manila envelope.

I opened the door. "What?"

His hatred was still smoldered, banked down. He held up
the envelope. "From Mr. B."

"Come in."

He entered, a few steps' worth, handed me the envelope.

"What is this?"

"Ten thousand."

"For what?"

"Mr. B's serious."

"Serious about what?"

"Come tomorrow at nine P.M. Talk to Mr. B. Forty more."

"Why doesn't he just call me?"

"I do everything for Mr. B."

"What do you do for Mrs. B?"

A finger jutted toward my chest. His voice was thick. "Stay away from her."

"You think she loves you, Arnuldo?"

His eyes widened in outrage. "Fuck you, Henry. Stay away from her."

He spun, walked out into the rain. He still hadn't figured it out. Maybe he never would. Lynette didn't love anyone. She didn't know how. It wasn't even her fault.

If you're not loved early enough, you're incapable of loving. You just don't understand what it is, you don't know what you're missing, nor can you conceive that you're missing anything.

I didn't know Lynette's history. Her real history. Maybe she didn't even know. But Mom and Dad, or whoever, had gone missing. She may have been treated kindly, but kindness is no substitute for love.

I hefted the envelope. Fifty was murder money. Artie wanted me to off Lynette. What else could it be?

I'd make the nine o'clock appointment. To return the ten and finally tell Artie to fuck off.

PART THREE

The Business
at Hand

CHAPTER FORTY

An Alibi Created

At a central table in Ruth's Chris Steak House, Judy Benjamin held court, surrounded by a coterie of her favorite acquaintances. She was dressed in a crimson, strapless gown that defied gravity. It was a jovial assemblage, well lubricated by preprandial cocaine and expensive dinner wine.

The fine steaks had been served but not all that much eating was being done. Which was fine with her. She pulled out her phone and fooled with it. It worked fine. But she didn't want a traceable call on her account. She tapped Vicky, in the next seat. Vicky was a producer with no credits. Which meant she was a caterer interrupted.

"What a great party," enthused Vicky, mindful of her situation and her hostess. Artie Benjamin wanted to help her, in more ways than one, so she was weighing her options, seeing where advantage lay.

"I need to borrow your phone for a second," said Judy. "My piece of shit isn't working."

Vicky handed over her phone, and Judy excused herself. In the ladies' lounge she dialed Jerry Shunk. He answered on the third ring.

"Hello?"

"Jerry. It's me." She could feel his heart leap half a mile up the street. Tiresome old fool. But some fools wrote wills.

"Judy? What is it?"

"Jerry." Pain and fright crept into her voice. "Something terrible has happened."

"What? What?"

"Artie's just given me papers."

"What kind of papers?"

"I don't know what kind of papers. But he laughed about them. They don't look funny."

"He can't give you any papers. I haven't written any."

"Jesus Christ, Jerry, he put some fucking papers in my hand. Are you going to help me or not?"

"Okay, okay. I'll take a look at them." He'd better take a look at them. Had Artie hired outside help? Nosy lawyers could be dangerous.

"You at Nate 'n Al's?"

"Like every Friday night."

"Can I send Arnuldo over?"

"Fine. I'll be finished in ten minutes."

Her voice sank into the softness of relief. "Thanks, Jerry. You're a lifesaver."

She clicked off. *Bingo.*

She dialed another number.

Arnuldo answered. "Yes."

"You ready?"

"Ready."

The line went dead. Good. Arnuldo was ready.

Which was another problem. Fucking Arnuldo was always ready. Always needy. She'd created another pest in her own home.

She futzed with her lipstick, went back to her guests.

"Thanks, hon." She gave Vicky her phone back. "How's your steak?"

"It's wonderful. Melts in your mouth almost."

Vicky pointed to Judy's untouched filet mignon. "What about yours? They forgot to cook it."

Lynette looked at the meat as if for the first time. "You're right." It was very rare. But she hadn't ordered it to eat it.

How do you want your steak? the waiter had asked, pulling a black enamel pen from his blue apron.

She had smiled. Blood rare.

That's very rare, ma'am.

And that's what I want. Slap it on the ass and run it through the kitchen.

Edgardo had shrugged. Maybe it was the full moon. But he had delivered the steak as ordered. *Slap it on the ass and run it through the kitchen.* Let's see you eat it.

The woman hadn't even tasted her steak. But lots of wine had gone down, and the bill would be significant. The wine was horse piss of Sardinian extraction that fell off the truck every Tuesday night between two and three with a French label around its neck. It moved briskly at sixty-four dollars a bottle. *Bueno*. Wine snobs. They'd praise Gallo if the bottle was nice.

Lynette looked around. At least the wine was good. The apex of the dinner hour had been reached. The dining room was full, people were waiting. The clattering, chattering din of happy, busy diners filled the air. She took a deep breath. Showtime.

She craned her head around, looking for her waiter, Egbardo or whatever his name was. Finally she caught his eye.

Over he came. "Yes, ma'am?"

She pointed at her steak. "Look at this steak."

"Yes, ma'am?" Certainly she wasn't going to complain about the way it had been cooked.

"This isn't what I ordered," she said in a loud voice. Other tablemates, hearing the timbre of confrontation, turned to see.

"It's rare, ma'am, like you wanted it," said Edgardo.

"This isn't how I wanted it at all." A flat definitive. And loud.

Other patrons turned to eye the lady in the red dress and her table of celebrants.

Edgardo had taken a lot of shit in his life. At this exact moment he was close to full up. "If I remember, ma'am"—you stupid white Westside cow—"you said 'Slap it on the ass and run it through the kitchen.'"

"Listen here, *Pancho,* I said nothing of the fucking kind."

She now commanded the complete attention of all the other patrons.

"My name is not Pancho, ma'am. My name is—"

"I don't fucking care what your name is—I want some goddam service around here. Get the manager."

Edgardo, red-faced, furious, retreated, met the manager coming across the dining room.

Walt Faulkner, new manager, hurried to table number 13. Obviously, there was a problem. As he arrived, the woman in the red dress got to her feet, tipping over her chair.

"Can I help you, ma'am?"

"Are you the fucking manager?"

"I'm the manager." There was a difference. "Can I help you?"

Judy pointed to the steak. "See that thing?"

Faulkner looked down on an extremely rare cut of fine, marbled beef. "I see rare beef."

"Is that all you see, *motherfucker*?" demanded the woman.

"Ma'am, if you don't tone it down, I'm going to have to ask you to—"

"Ask me to leave?" shouted Judy. "You're going to ask me to leave? My question is this."

The restaurant was utterly silent.

"Excuse me, ma'am, but you're really going to have—"

She cut him off like a Hummer would a Subaru at a four-way stop. "My question is this, meat whistle. Why can't a girl get good beef in Beverly Hills?"

Whereupon Judy reached down to her plate, picked up the filet with her bare hand, drew it back like a baseball, and threw it, full force.

All eyes followed the sanguinary missile as it sailed across the dining room and hit Elizabeth Grimble square in the forehead. It hung there for a second, then plopped onto her bread plate.

There was a stunned silence. Judy picked up her chair, sat down, shrugged, sipped her water. Mission accomplished.

The avalanche of laughter was heard up and down Beverly Drive.

CHAPTER FORTY-ONE

The Lord Laughs at Us All

I left early for Benjamin's so I could kill two birds with one stone. At Gardner and Hollywood I stopped at St. Paul of Tarsus, rang the bell at the residence. Reverend Jenkins opened the door, invited me in.

As before, I was shown into the library and made comfortable. Reverend Jenkins again looked into the depths of my soul. "How are you, Mr. Henry?" he asked.

I said I was fine, that I had a check for the mission I somehow didn't feel comfortable giving to his assistant. I finished on an up note, hoping aloud that he had not lost his keys again.

The reverend laughed. "I've got my keys, Mr. Henry, it's my cell phone I've lost."

I laughed and he laughed.

"But it's funny you mention Mr. Linscomb."

I tried to look blank.

"Mr. Linscomb quit his position."

"Really."

"Out of the blue. Two days ago."

"He left a note?"

"No. He just cleared out his things and disappeared. I called the parish in Santa Barbara where he'd come from to see if they'd heard from him. Reverend Wells said they'd never heard of him. *Ever.* Quite extraordinary, really."

"Maybe you should check the silver."

"I did."

"And?"

The reverend shrugged. "I checked and rechecked. Then I realized I didn't know what was there to begin with."

I liked Reverend Jenkins a lot. I fished out my donation envelope, handed it to him. "So what's your cell number?"

He told me. "I go to bed pretty early," he cautioned. "But if you need an appointment . . ."

I dialed his number.

"Did you just call *me,* Mr. Henry?"

"Yes, I did."

I could see he thought I'd lost my marbles in the war. "But— I'm right here."

I smiled at him. "You think I'm crazy."

"Are you?" A worried expression played over his face.

"No. But I got lucky with your keys. I thought maybe I'd get lucky with your phone, too."

"I see," he said, plainly not seeing.

Then a cell phone rang. Muffled. He looked sharply around the room, then patted himself down, found his phone.

He was delighted. "Aha. My *other* pocket." He pulled out the phone, looked at me, nodded happily. "Excuse me a second." He answered his phone. "Hello?"

It was my turn to wonder.

Serious as a heart attack, not looking at me, the reverend spoke into the phone. "Is that you . . . Mr. Henry?"

Then he turned to me, reading my expression, almost exploding with mirth.

We laughed and laughed.

"It's the only way to get through life, Mr. Henry. Humor. How the Lord must laugh at us all."

How indeed.

CHAPTER FORTY-TWO

A Sack of Beets

Jerry Shunk and his accountant, Lucky Lee Feldman, had just stepped out of Nate 'n Al's delicatessen when they were hailed by a man in a blue peacoat. All Lucky's ventures turned gold.

"Jerry Shunk?" said the man.

Lucky turned first. Artie Benjamin's Sig Sauer P250 allowed the shooter to change the weapon's configuration at will. Caliber and size. Arnuldo had small hands. He had removed the functional mechanism and changed the weapon from a full size to subcompact. The 9-millimeter projectile hit Feldman right between the eyes and killed him instantly.

It took a second for Arnuldo to realize he'd made a mistake. The dead man was not old enough. He turned to Shunk.

Shunk moaned, his tongue incapable of speech, his hands vaguely waving. Arnuldo straightened his arm, shot Shunk through his right eye, another Moe Greene shot, dropping him like a sack of beets. Then Arnuldo walked to the corner, turned, calmly walked to the Mercedes on Canon Drive.

The Mercedes started up first time, every time. He drove quietly up to Santa Monica Boulevard, made a left turn. In fifteen minutes he'd hit the 405. Then he'd head north. Seven miles later he'd transfer to the 101. Then he'd let the fine German engine have its way. Next stop Big Sur.

CHAPTER FORTY-THREE

Hammerfall

For many years, for ten years, working with Mr. Benjamin had been good. Until Mrs. Benjamin had become Judy. From that moment it was inevitable that he would climb the stairs with a new mission in mind.

Benjamin barely looked up from his desk. "Where you been? Fucking Bill Robertson. Doesn't want to pay for the camera he ruined. I think you're going to have to pay him a visit. Over on Varna. Asshole."

At this point Arnuldo would usually ask how much pressure to exert and where to exert it. But this time the Filipino said nothing. Just looked at him calmly.

"We gotta pay Robertson a visit. Got that?"

Arnuldo nodded. Oh, I got that. "Got it. Boss." Boss. This asshole, who treated Judy so rudely, so faithlessly, was BOSS.

Benjamin looked over another piece of paper, then sharply up at Arnuldo. "Something wrong today? Don't seem like yourself."

"I'm not sure what you mean, Mr. B."

Benjamin had always liked Arnuldo referring to him as Mr. B. It showed that not only was he the boss but he was respected and liked at the same time. And why wouldn't he be liked and respected? He paid the little brown son of a bitch twenty-five hundred a week straight under the table. That was ten grand a month. A hundred and twenty a year.

Artie Benjamin was a fair and generous man. More than fair, magnanimous. One day, maybe he would get over to Manila like he'd always said he would and check it out. Why not? Manila was an international city. And Arnuldo had told him an amazing fact. Well, maybe it was a fact. Filipino women grew no hair on their legs. They didn't need to shave. They didn't have that fucked-up American stubble.

And even the American women—at least they weren't Europeans with hair everywhere.

That woman in Paris. She didn't have a thatch, which was bad enough, she had a goddam mop. And more hair under her arms than he did. Fur on her back. Neanderthal. That wasn't right. Thank God for that shitty French wine. It had given him a forward momentum nothing could stop.

Manila. Why not, really? Maybe he could set up a franchise sort of idea. The Fellatio Academy was up and running. He was going to make a goddam fortune. But, hey, what about *The Manila Fellatio Academy?* Had a ring to it. *The Paris Fellatio Academy.* Not that they needed an academy over there. But the title might stiffen a cock or two in Dubuque. Or Idaho Falls.

He emerged from his thoughts to see Arnuldo playing with that gun. The gun was adjustable or something, you could switch this and that. "How do you like that gun, Arnuldo?"

"I like it just fine, Mr. Benjamin."

There was something wrong. Maybe it was time to lay down a little law. "I don't know what your problem is, Arnuldo, but what the fuck, here?"

Arnuldo shrugged.

The son of a bitch shrugged. *Shrugged!*

"What the hell, Arnuldo? You got a problem with the chow I provide around here? Your rooms? Or the car you drive, or what? What is it?"

"Fuck you, Mr. Benjamin."

The sound of Arnuldo's voice was flat and cold and Benjamin suddenly realized Arnuldo was not playing with the gun. The hand that held the weapon was wrapped in a plastic fruit bag from Ralphs. Benjamin's throat went suddenly dry. He held up a mediating hand. "W-w-wait a second."

"Good-bye, Mr. Benjamin."

Arnuldo pulled the trigger. Sig Sauer quality. Smooth and even pull. He felt the solid, metallic click of hammerfall and the bilateral impact of the report on his eardrums.

It was a Moe Greene shot, through Mr. B's right eye. A hole in one. Through the blue haze, Arnuldo saw brains all over the place.

Arnuldo's cell phone rang. That would be Judy. From the steak house. Of course he was ready.

CHAPTER FORTY-FOUR

Like a Bowling Pin

In order to aid riffraff suppression, there was no neighborhood parking in Beverly Hills after 6:00 P.M. without permit. But I was only going to be there long enough to give Benjamin his latest money back. I left my flashers on, went up to the house, and rang.

I heard the four-note chime from deep in the house and waited. A composer I had known defined melody as the departure *from* and the return *to* home. The four notes of a doorbell were supposedly the second simplest example of that hypothesis.

The composer had choked to death on a ham sandwich. What was important was that no one was coming to the door. I checked my watch. I was right on time.

I rang again, waited. Then I noticed the front door was slightly ajar. I pushed and it opened up.

Normal subdued evening lights were on, but I stepped into dead silence. "Hello? Hel-lo?"

No echo, no nothing. "Mr. Benjamin? Mr. Benjamin?"

I started getting that feeling I get. Its onset is so subtle I don't know where it begins. All of a sudden I have it and my skin is crawling.

I walked quietly into the living room. Again, nothing. And

nothing in the dining room. In the distance I heard the wail of a siren. Some sucker going down.

"Mr. Benjamin," I called strongly. Nothing.

Then I went up the stairs and caught a whiff. Nitrocellulose and nitroglycerin. Gunpowder.

I walked to his office. The smell was strong. I flipped on the lights.

That blue-gray haze in the air. Benjamin in his chair. But his right eye was an oozing hole and his brains had been blown out. There was money all over his desk. Suddenly I realized that the siren was close.

Then many sirens and the screech of brakes. And here I was, at the scene of the crime, standing in someone's brains, set up like a bowling pin. Time to get truckin'.

Downstairs, people burst in. I tossed Arnuldo's ten thousand into the mix on Artie's desk. I wasn't going to be the rat in this trap. I took three sticky steps past Benjamin to the window, pushed it open. There was a tree, but too far to reach. There was a drainpipe. It was that or nothing. I went down hand over hand, leaving footprints on the wall, dropped into the bushes.

I headed for the back of the property. All homes in the neighborhood bordered an alley. No riffraff trash cans out by the front curb. I heard the hubbub from the house and saw lights flashing around, but it was quiet where I was. I went over the back wall into some thorny ferns.

I waited. Silence. I'd have to call Rojas.

I stepped out of the ferns, tried to stroll like a millionaire. Three steps later I saw a glint of light in a moving shadow and the lights went out.

CHAPTER FORTY-FIVE

Peedner Remembers

Lieutenant Lew Peedner had known this day was coming. And now here it was. Dick Henry arrested. But the joy he had anticipated at the arrest had not materialized. Instead, a deep, gray depression. From the roots of his hair down through his fingernails.

The memories of the night in question had never left him. A night that had truncated his future, left him limping and damaged, forever shackled to the past.

He and Henry had been partners. It had been a good fit. Their skills and liabilities offset one another. The cowboy and the accountant. The sword and the pen. Shortcut Man and Bo Peep. Dick broke all the rules and Lew could enumerate Dick's offenses, chapter, subchapter, and verse. And file the reports that got them promotions, put their actions into lawful perspective.

Over time, the arc of Dick's behavior had swung wider and wider, and Lew had responded with genuine creative authorship. He knew it couldn't last, shouldn't last, that trouble was coming. But he couldn't break it off. Their lives had grown together. He had been to Dick and Georgette's wedding, Dick and Georgette had come to his and Marilyn's. He warned Dick, in explicit terms, *this was a new world,* but Dick didn't get it.

The administrative ground had changed beneath their boots, but the fool hadn't seen it.

The soju, sweet potato cousin of vodka, was flowing in Koreatown that payday Friday night when the call came in. A little girl, Soon Cha Kim, eight, had gone missing.

He and Dick, working out of Wilshire Station, had rolled over. The parents were frantic, the language barrier formidable. They ran a little video shop at Olympic and Western. They worked fourteen hours a day. Usually sixteen. Sometimes eighteen.

The family lived in a three-story brick walk-up on the south side of Twelfth Street half a block east of Western. The girl's instructions were to come home promptly after school, lock the door, and admit no one. But someone had been admitted. Her parents found the door unlocked, the apartment undisturbed.

None of the neighbors had seen anything.

Nobody had come in or out since the girl came home from school?

Nobody.

Nobody?

Nobody. Well, the usual villains. The mailman. Domino's. Regular visitors.

And there was that man with the bag.

Dick's ears pricked up. Man with a bag?

Delivery dude, I guess.

What kind of bag?

You saw him, too, said one neighbor to another. Like a big duffel bag. Green. Green canvas.

Maybe, I dunno. I didn't see nothin'. I guess he coulda been carryin' somethin'.

What was in the bag? asked Dick.

Look. Maybe it wasn't a bag. But it was a green canvas something. It looked kinda heavy when he left.

When he left? What made you think it was heavy?

Dude leaned to one side when he carried it.

Dick looked at Peedner, made the inductive leap. "Sounds like Elton Reese."

"Elton Reese is in CSP Sacramento."

"Maybe he isn't."

He wasn't.

They'd released him from ad seg CSP twenty-two days earlier. Notes formalized his good behavior and indicated he'd accepted Jesus as his personal savior.

Reese had a long sheet. The usual adolescent beefs, truancy, petty theft, possession, under the influence. But mixed in were disturbing crimes. Setting dogs and cats on fire. And then, with adulthood, and other serious crimes, he'd graduated to the torture of human beings. Children. He had a particular m.o. He'd carry off his young victims, bound and gagged, in bags, in boxes, in sacks. He'd been caught only once. That's why he's been sent to CSP Sacramento. Three missing kids had been credited to his informal account.

The only positive element noted in Reese's entire life was winning a fifth-grade piano competition.

Lew and Dick called in Eddie Wilkins and Bob Herbert to finish taking the report.

Dick put the pedal to the metal. Using lights but no siren, they sped down Western, turned right on Venice, right on South Manhattan Place.

At one time South Manhattan Place must have been *the* place to live. Huge old Craftsman homes, eight, nine, ten bedrooms. Built in the time when families were *families,* not mom and dad, 2.2 brats, and a parakeet.

But now, fifty years of diminishing returns had transformed these old houses into slovenly, sagging eyesores, reroofed forty times, orange showing through green showing through black, divided up into dingy warrens.

Harold Crownes, Reese's uncle, had owned the third house on the left.

They knocked, but there was no response. Dick kicked the door in, met Crownes coming toward the door.

"What the fu——?" spluttered the old man. Then Dick had him by the throat, off his feet, against the greasy paneling.

"Where's Elton?"

Crownes, hanging, spread his hands, shook his head a little bit.

"Where's fucking Elton?" Dick shouted, veins on his neck and forehead in sharp relief.

"Set the man down so he can talk, Dick."

Dick dropped him. "Where the fuck is Elton?"

"Dunno where he at."

Then, from somewhere upstairs, they heard a long, thin scream.

Dick hit Crownes with a straight overhand right and smashed his face.

They raced up the stairs, and Lew was at Dick's heels till he slipped. By the time he got to the third floor he'd heard four shots.

The four shots that had ruined his life.

CHAPTER FORTY-SIX

The Unfairness of Life

Walt Faulkner did not expect to be fired. But after six days as the new night manager of Ruth's Chris Steak House on Beverly Drive, he did have a bad feeling when Roger Hanberry, district supervisor, requested to meet with him a couple of days after the debacle. Still, how bad could things be?

Plenty bad.

Not only was one customer, Elizabeth Grimble, suing for battery and humiliation but the food fight that followed had been the only known food fight in Ruth's Chris history. And possibly one of the more expensive food fights since the days of Nero.

Seventy-nine-dollar steaks had flown around the room like UFOs at Roswell. Followed by chicken, ribs, assorted seafood, and bread. Flatware, stemware, and furniture had been pulverized, and in the panic that ensued the majority of customers had fled, though stampeded would be a better word. The great majority did not pay their bills. Eighty-three customers had claimed injury. Three hundred and thirteen had called to complain of ruined clothing, though the restaurant seated only 170 guests. Sixty-two complete sets of silverware had wandered into the street all by themselves, never to be seen again, and another thirty-nine sets had pieces missing. The carpet and subcarpeting were ruined and would have to be replaced from wall to wall. Some fixtures in the restrooms had been destroyed. Corporate attorneys predicted total losses approaching $700,000.

Faulkner had said not a word. None of this could have been foreseen; there was nothing he could have done to stop it after it began.

"And I am told," intoned Hanberry gravely, "that you called one of our customers a meat whistle."

That bitch.

"No, sir," said Faulkner, speaking at last. "It was the customer who called *me* a meat whistle."

Hanberry straightened his papers, stood up. "The customer is always right, Faulkner. You're fired."

Someone was going to fall on his sword. It was not going to be Roger C. Hanberry.

CHAPTER FORTY-SEVEN

Music Lessons Lost

Peedner was in no rush. They'd kept the son of a bitch over-night just for drill. Now, at his order, they'd brought him up to the interrogation room. Peedner looked through the one-way glass.

Henry, Richard Hudson, forty-three, not only smelled of gunpowder, he was covered with blood. On his hands, on his shoes, on his knees. And his fingerprints were all over the room in question, the drainpipe, on the wall he'd scaled down.

No weapon had been found. Not yet. But he had been caught trying to escape. In the alley behind the house.

Ferguson came up, handed Peedner some papers. "It's Ben-jamin's blood all over him."

Peedner looked at the lab results. "Thanks, Tom."

Again he peered through the one-way glass. Henry was handcuffed, partially illuminated by the single shaded over-head lamp throwing down a narrow cone of light.

Some philosophies held there were no accidents. That what a man allowed was no different than what he caused. East-ern bullshit. Yet, if he'd gotten rid of the fucking Sundance Kid when he'd known Dick was slipping out of control—

Fuck that. Dick shouldn't have been out of control. Or did he mean Butch Cassidy?

Peedner entered interrogation room 3. It was a large, square room, twenty-five feet on a side with a high ceiling. Sound echoed all around, and his footsteps reverberated as he stopped in the grit on the floor.

Henry didn't even turn around. "That you, Lew?"

Peedner couldn't help the gloating tone that entered his speech. "It sure is, Dick."

"I didn't do it."

"Of course not." Peedner walked around the table, looked down at his old partner. "Benjamin's blood all over you, that's just a coincidence."

"You assholes kept me here all night."

"What do we assholes know? We're just cops."

"You know me."

"You smell like gunpowder, Dick."

"I went into a room where a man had just been shot. You know I wouldn't just kill someone."

"Maybe he needed killing." Peedner stared into Henry's eyes. He couldn't keep the bitterness out of his voice.

"If only Elton Reese had been a white man, Lew."

Yes. If only Elton Reese had been a white man. Then it would have been commendation time. Lew and I would've been heroes. And Lew would have long since been a captain.

I had broken a cop's primary unwritten directive: Never get personally involved. Police work is a team effort. Let the team do its thing. Just do your little part and forget about the big picture. Justice is abstract, not concrete, not your concern.

But I'd never been able to forget Elton Reese and the lives he'd destroyed. The fact that he'd been sentenced to California

State Prison at Sacramento was not satisfactory. Though after a while I'd allowed it to slip out of mind.

When the Twelfth Street witness mentioned the bag, it all came back. I knew it was Reese. And I remembered where he had lived before prison.

The findings of the board were stark and unemotional. In three minutes I'd reduced the codebook to pulp.

As far as Harold Crownes was concerned, I'd crushed his alveolar process and shattered his maxilla. And knocked out most of his upper teeth at the same time. They made a big deal out of the fact that he was sixty-three. Soon Cha Kim was eight.

In the matter of Elton Reese, the board decided I'd taken matters into my own hands. I made no apologies. And I make no apologies. They were right. I was filled with an unprofessional, biblical rage. Moses did not come down the mountain and file a grievance report. He smashed the evil he beheld.

When I heard that scream, I took the stairs two at a time until I reached the third floor.

I found Reese in a small, front-facing room, filthy, illuminated by a dim bulb on a wire and some candles. Garbage was all over the place. Beer cans, pizza boxes. He looked up at me from his position on the floor, near the wall.

Pants around his knees, he knelt between the legs of little Soon Cha Kim. His half-erect cock dangled, red, and in his right hand was a small knife. The little girl was motionless, one arm to her side, the other flung over her head. I didn't know if she were alive or dead. There was blood all over.

Reese looked up at me, raised his hands in the air, and grinned. *Grinned.* "I guess you got me, lawman. I surrender," he said. Then he shrugged.

I don't know if it was the grin or the shrug. My first bullet pierced the frontal bone of his skull above his right eye and exited through the left occipital bone. The force of that round turned his head to the left as it went through.

The second bullet penetrated the glabella, where the cranium knits at the center of the forehead. Because the second bullet entered at a thirty-degree angle, it did not make exit but instead ricocheted round and round inside the skull, plowing through lots of tissue. His music lessons were gone before he hit the deck. The third and fourth bullets were superfluous. The third through the left sphenoid bone, the fourth through the left temporal bone.

That's what they hung me on. The first two might have had legal justification, lethal threat, imminent danger. But three and four were personal. And cops don't get personal. They just take care of business.

Further examinations almost proved that the vicious kick he'd received to his face, shattering his chin, scattering his teeth, and dislocating his jaw, had been rendered posthumously.

That was all they wrote for me. Judges, juries, and executioners usually constitute three separate departments. I should have received the Edwin P. Smallwood Los Angeles County Municipal Efficiency Prize. Oh, well.

Instead, the world was informed that the reprehensible actions committed, and the Cro-Magnon who'd committed them had no place in modern Los Angeles law enforcement. My admin leave was canceled and I was encouraged to retire and I did. I shook a lot of hands on the way out.

Soon Cha Kim survived. Now she'd be twenty-two or twenty-three, I guess. I hope she's long forgotten my name and the reasons she might remember it.

Lew was a different story. He was a third-generation cop and had nowhere to go and a baby on the way. I told the board he had nothing to do with any of my actions. But community activists made hay, and matters of blood, long diluted, returned full strength. Lew accepted reprimand and was reduced in rank. And it had been a hard road for him ever since. I knew he hated me. I didn't blame him.

The hard decisions in life are not often clear choices between black and white. They are between white and off-white, between black and dark gray. And so, between expunging Elton Reese and maintaining Lew's career trajectory, my decision had been instinctive, instantaneous.

There was a knock at the door, and another officer entered the room, handed papers to Lew, turned around, and left.

That would probably be my negative GSR.

Lew frowned. It was my negative GSR.

Lew rubbed his face. "Okay, Dick. So what do you know about Artie Benjamin?"

"Can we undo the cuffs, here?"

Lew unlocked them and blood rushed, pins and needles, back into my hands.

"What do you know about Benjamin?"

I'd had time to think about everything. As they hauled me to the station in the rat wagon. I'd waited for ball four and taken strike three. And I'd known better. Lynette had set me up. Pure and simple.

Had I loved her? Yes. We had our brief stay in paradise. Had she loved me? Yes. *Yes*. As best she could. I would always believe it.

Now there was nothing.

What did all this make me?

Someone who cast a long shadow at sundown, someone with the infinite capability to fool himself, someone indistinguishable from the most ordinary and fallible of men.

"So what do I know about Benjamin?" I laughed and part of me died.

A couple of hours later they cut me loose. I felt like a public moron, but it was a nice afternoon; it was warm and the sun came down. The long, straight lines of my Cadillac cheered me up a bit. I went home, took a long shower, changed clothes.

Who killed Jerry Shunk and the other lawyer? Follow the money. Benjamin dies, Lynette inherits. With a Shunk document aiding and abetting. For a piece, of course. And who knew the full dimension of payment? No doubt the fool had a dream. So Jerry's ticket was punched and his claim set aside permanently. Hell, I was surprised she didn't ask me to do the job. For a piece after probate. Most likely she hadn't gotten around to it.

Which left Arnuldo. Unless there was someone else with his beak in the pie, Arnuldo was doing her killing. And if that were true, his days were numbered as well, he was a loose end, he was playing on the freeway. I hoped a Cadillac wouldn't have to run him down.

Lynette, spider woman, had a plan. At some point, there would be a last man standing. Then that last man would have an accident. She would play the innocent beauty card and bluff her way through.

I picked up the *Times* at the Country Store. The paper was thin as a widow. The big story was the murder spree in Beverly Hills. Upstanding citizens pined for days of yore and John Wayne justice. The stricken widow, Judy Benjamin, had gone into seclusion. An unidentified man had been questioned and released.

Cool. I was famous in a nonfamous way. But seclusion had an address. Big Sur.

CHAPTER FORTY-EIGHT

Franklin Closes the Deal

As he walked into St. Paul of Tarsus Church on Sunday morning, Franklin Tillman's eye was caught by a white 1969 Cadillac Coupe de Ville convertible crossing Gardner, heading east on Hollywood. He'd owned one just like it. For a second he wondered if he were in the Cadillac. Maybe he was. Time was all mixed up. But then he was back on the steps. He entered the church.

The letter he had received from Francie's brother had crushed him in a way he had never imagined.

Dear Mr. Franklin,

I am writing you on behalf my sister, Francie. I have terrible news. Francie was killed in accident last week coming home from hospital visiting our sister. She was crossing Rojas Blvd in central Manila when a truck no brakes hit her. She was thrown long distance and landed very hurtful. She was conscious but no pain then she died. Before she passed she spoke me her love from you and she said she would carry that love to the Lord. Francie want very much be your wife. A priest on the street gave her last rites. Then she went to the Lord. I know she loved you very much because she mentioned you often. I wish I am not the bearing of such sad news. She will be buried in her home province, Nueva Ecija, tomorrow. Prayers to you. She said you loved the Lord.

Sincerely,

Alfonso D. Corro

Franklin had been married forty years. The relationship had been difficult. He had done the right thing, raising his family, sticking the marriage out. That's what a man did.

He had no idea what love was. Perhaps a transitory condition necessary to launch your ship, a billion other ships. Perhaps a condition best appreciated from afar. Up close, his marriage had been a wan neutrality, the company of an intimate stranger.

Then Abigail had died. His great secret was his relief, communicated to no one. He saw things more clearly now; she had been a good woman. If only she'd married someone she loved. He wasn't glad she was gone, but he didn't miss her, either.

And then the miracle of Francie. The glorious miracle of Francie's love, Francie's regard, her peculiar Filipino sense of humor and choice of words.

That old line of bullshit, you're only as old as you feel, had been revealed as the truth. He made his muscle in the mirror. And goddam, there was still something there! Still something there!

He wanted to dance, he wanted to see plays, he wanted to see films, he wanted to hear music, he bought a bicycle at Pep Boys even though the cute little Mexican girl at the check stand told him he'd kill himself.

Then the letter from her brother. Francie. Dead. Run down on the streets of Manila. Dying right there as the world gawked, as the jitneys jostled noisily through traffic.

He had never cried like that before in his life. Not when his dad went, not when his mother went two years later.

Oh, Dad, said Betty, putting her arms around him as the tears rolled down the eroded channels of his face. Age, so recently lifted from his shoulders, fell heavily back.

Dr. Nguyen had prescribed something to ease anxiety, but he had thrown the pills away when Betty left. Taking those medications would erase Francie. Would diminish the size of her loss, reduce the clarity of his suffering.

He had been unable to sleep, try as he might. Day for night, night for day, it was all jumbled up and then the radio said it was Sunday. Time for church. But with his confusion came a peculiar sense, that for the first time in his life, his prayers had weight, had substance, that someone was actively listening. After long negotiations, he had hammered out a deal with the Creator. It was preposterous and against all reason. Reversing time's arrow. It was a deal only the Creator could honor.

Lord, grant Francie her life and take mine. Grant Francie her life and take mine. Grant Francie her life and take mine. Grant Francie her life and take mine.

Somehow, the circularity of this thought provided comfort for him and rendered the impossible possible. When he'd greeted Reverend Jenkins that morning, Francie's mantra underlay the conversation, resuming stature at pauses in the flow of words. Reverend Jenkins's brains had about fallen out. He was always losing things. He'd lost his car at the car wash. *Grant Francie her life and take mine. Grant Francie her life and take mine.*

At the Consecration of the Mass, when the Eucharist was held high for the world to see His triumph—*grant Francie her life and take mine*—Franklin had felt a twinge in his neck. He had turned his head to the right, then to the left to clear his discomfort. As he looked left, he saw Francie across the aisle, two rows back. There was no doubt in his heart.

A great force rose up and thrust him to his feet in exclamation. "JOY! JOY! JOY!" he cried, neck corded, his voice ringing around the nave, staring at his beloved, unquestionably alive. The deal had gone through! As promised! He took one step toward her and suddenly he was on the marble floor, staring up into a circle of faces.

And there she was! There she was! Gazing down at him with utter tenderness, the tenderness he had searched for his entire life. He reached his hand toward her, it seemed to take forever, pushing through thick air, but he got there and she took it between her own. She smelled of jasmine.

Josefina Reyes Corro, a food service worker at the Manila mission, looked down on the old man. Who did he think she was? That he had died loving her, loving her very personally, his eyes startlingly blue and penetrating, was beyond doubt.

Miss Corro would remember this moment her entire life and would never fail to offer a prayer for the old gentleman who had unaccountably loved her so.

Though her trip to the United States had been funded by the Hollywood congregation in return for twenty devoted years of service to the mission, she would always believe that the Lord had sent her to Los Angeles to hold Mr. Tillman's hand as he passed into the Presence. How dearly she loved the Lord. How dearly she loved the Lord.

CHAPTER FORTY-NINE

Arnuldo Goes Down to the Beach

The Pacific rolled toward Hawaii and she watched it go. Only a thousand people lived in Big Sur, she knew three of them, they worked at the store, already she was bored. But a good bored. She inhaled her Virginia Slim.

Artie was gone. Never again would she have to look up into those hairy nostrils while he lay atop her, huffing and puffing, the little engine that could, conveying a nut to the top of the hill.

What would she miss? Moments. Moments here and there. Moments at the beginnings of things, when she didn't know who he really was. When he was a Las Vegas impresario, winning awards, important.

She heard clattering from the kitchen. Arnuldo, audibly pouting. How much attention could she pay?

She flicked her cigarette over the side, watched it fall until it disappeared about halfway down. What had Artie said? Two hundred and eleven feet, give or take something or other. And if you squared a and divided or multiplied times b, you found it took three seconds to reach the rocks. Then there was something called terminal velocity, but that didn't figure in until . . . until something.

She'd underestimated her growing disinterest in Arnuldo. In the fog of events, she'd imagined dropping him off some comfortable distance down the road. With a nice piece of change. And her gratitude. And that would be it. But now she was feeling impatient.

Men. What was it with them? From Caesar the emperor to Cesar the busboy. They really wanted just one thing. To be pedestaled and adored. And blown. That wasn't going to happen. Adoration, anyway.

The screen door slid open and shut, Arnuldo appeared, set his butterfly knife on the railing, lit up a Viceroy.

He gazed on her perfection. They had made love last night but his mind had not been free.

Sharing Judy with Mr. Benjamin had been barely tolerable. Now Mr. Benjamin was at rest. But Henry? To allow his mind even to drift into that vicinity caused a red rage and a bright pain that twisted him physically.

The tender words she and Henry had whispered when they lay in the night. How she had touched him. What she had allowed, what she had entertained, what she had initiated. As if he, Arnuldo, had never walked the face of the earth. Henry would die. Slowly.

And Judy? The conclusion slid smoothly out of his subconscious, a ticket from an automatic kiosk. Death. Death would cleanse dishonor. He watched the tide smash onto the rocks below. He would kiss her a last time, then commend her to the sea.

"This place is very beautiful," said Arnuldo, looking over the blueness. "But one day I will show you Baguio."

Oh no, you won't. "Baguio. Where's Baguio again?"

"In the mountains of Luzon."

"In the Philippines."

"Of course, in the Philippines." Arnuldo spat a shred of tobacco over the cliff. Long way down.

"I can't wait."

Arnuldo shaded his eyes, stared at her.

What the fuck was with Arnuldo? All she needed was for him to go off. Kill a store clerk for cigarettes. "I'm sorry, Arnuldo. I haven't been me. All this pressure. Artie told me he was going to have you killed."

"No way."

"But it scared me."

He watched her turn and walk away from him, to the far corner of the large wooden deck. Her back was to him, shoulders shaking.

He felt himself filled with a noble sympathy. He walked over, put his stone hand on her shoulder. *A last kiss.* She turned to him, her eyes the color of the ocean on a misty day. "I love you so much, baby girl," he said.

But the howling vacuum had opened up inside her again, with its endless vistas of nothingness and no return, the harlequinade of grasping, painted lovers. Within the arms that reached to gather her close, she lowered her head, rammed it into Arnuldo's face. That stood him up. He staggered backward. She followed him, quick as a cat, gave him a two-handed shove.

He hit the rail, pinwheeled for balance. *Judy.* Then he went over.

Time decelerated to a new constant, he was barely moving, he had all the time in the world, looking up at the sky, seeing those majestic blues and grays high above streaked with lacy tatters of cloud. He had a clear choice to scream but why bother? From his first moments of awareness in Tondo to the rocks calling him from below—all a string of specifically fashioned, inevitably connected events, a rosary of time and space with only one possible conclusion. He thought he heard his mother's voice and then . . .

What she needed was a cigarette. She lit up. The Pacific stretched away. A couple of thousand miles to Oahu.

CHAPTER FIFTY

To Slay a Prince

I arrived on Paseo de Pacific, shut down the Caddy, walked back to Benjamin's house. Lucky bastard. It must have cost him seven, eight million. Not that lucky, I guess.

There were two cars in the open garage. Lynette's Jaguar and a midsize blue Mercedes. Arnuldo had come up, too. The police in L.A. were looking high and low for him.

The front door was off the latch. I took the safety off my Korth 9 millimeter, $2,500 worth of fine German gunsmithing. I went in, called out, but no answer.

There were dishes on the kitchen table. Two settings. An ashtray. Two brands. Had to be Arnuldo. He'd be dangerous as a snake. I went to the window that gave onto the deck. There she was. Alone. Where was the Inside Man? The house was silent.

I pushed the door open, and she turned around.

As always, her beauty hit me like a sledgehammer. She must have been very close to my personal ideal. My emotional side opened a wide door for excuses, lies, and fictions. But I wasn't going there.

"Where's Arnuldo?"

"You're here to see Arnuldo?"

"Where is he?"

"He went down to the beach. What did you come up here for?"

"To see you."

She spread her hands, invited me to gaze. "Here I am, slake your thirst." A wide smile, innocent as the dawn.

I looked, really looked at her. Pitch-black hair framed those green eyes set in porcelain with dark freckles. The most beautiful human being I'd ever known. And with all that, all the tools to slay a prince, much less a man like me, with all that she'd turned evil.

My justifiable rage had bled out on Highway 1, and seeing her brought on a deep melancholy. Mood indigo. Yeah, Mr. Ellington knew the blues.

"What's with you, Dick? You're looking at me like a basset hound."

"I know I'm not going to be seeing you for a long time."

"Why? Where are you going?"

"It's where you're going, darling."

"And where am I going?"

"You're going to prison."

That hit close to home. "For what, may I ask?"

"You don't think they blamed Artie on me, do you? They'll be drawing up a case on you. For Jerry Shunk. For Lee Feldman. And for Artie."

"I don't know Lee Feldman."

"I don't think Arnuldo knew him, either."

"My alibis are airtight, Dick. For all those men."

"They better be blood tight, too."

Her voice took on that scornful tone. "What did you come up here for, Dick? To make a citizen's arrest?"

She was sagging in on herself. The oxygen was leaking out of her soul, her world was growing heavier. I could see it.

"No. I came up to tell you how sorry I am. Because we had it for a while, you and me. We had it. But it takes two to believe, and you never had the guts. Now there's nothing."

"Don't make me puke." Suddenly a butterfly knife was in her hand and she was coming at me. The blade whispered through the air.

And again.

And again. This time I stuck my foot out as she went by. She tripped, hit the railing. The railing fell away. Her momentum carried her right over.

I thought she was gone but she wasn't.

She was looking up at me, holding on with one hand, suspended over the abyss from a thick root just under the decking. I dived under the railing, grabbed the post, held on, reached down. "Grab my wrist with your other hand."

But she didn't.

"Grab my wrist."

She asked me a question instead. "Do you love me, Dick?"

"Grab my wrist, goddam you."

She took hold of it with a lunge. Then with both hands. Braced her feet against the face of the cliff, stared up at me.

"Do you love me, Dick?"

I tried to pull her up, she wouldn't come.

"*Do you love me,* Dick?"

"Noooo," I shouted, lying, pulling with all my strength.

Those emerald eyes stared into my marrow.

Then she let go.

Acknowledgments

Andrew C. Rigrod, Esq., Paul Pompian, Mace Neufeld—you guys were there in the great darkness before the earth was formed. Thank you.

Ryan Fischer-Harbage and Nicole Robson at the Fischer-Harbage Agency—you guys turned the magic key, and I'll always be grateful for your efforts.

To Anna de Vries and the staff at Scribner—your patient and cheerful suggestions made this book better. I crawled, I stood, I limped, and finally I walked. Thank you.

To all copy editors everywhere: no man is a hero to his valet, and no author a hero to his copy editor. Thank you for your excruciating attention to detail—my book is much improved for your efforts.

All lyrics courtesy of Pearly King, www.pearlykingmusic.com.

About the Author

p. g. sturges was born in Hollywood, California. Punctuated by fitful intervals of school, he has subsequently occupied himself as a submarine sailor, a Christmas tree farmer, a dimensional and optical metrologist, a writer, and a musician.

Read on for an excerpt from p. g. sturges's next novel,

TRIBULATIONS OF THE SHORTCUT MAN

coming in February 2012 from Scribner.

CHAPTER ONE

WHITE FOOLS WITH DREADLOCKS

Loman London believed the labors of others should profit Loman London. I had been summoned to disabuse him, again, of this quaint notion.

A soft Los Angeles morning sun gentled my shoulders as I made a left turn in my '69 Cadillac Coupe de Ville convertible from Ocean Avenue to Abbot Kinney Boulevard.

Kiyoko was on my mind. My on-and-off girlfriend, Kiyoko was a Buddhist who hadn't yet come to appreciate my line of work. Last night, to the accompaniment of Japanese imprecations, she'd thrown me out of her house. It didn't help that I'd laughed at her insults. I couldn't help it. I understood only a few words of Japanese. Forku, steaku, porku, elephanto. Americanized additions to the language. Not the words she had chosen from the other side of the kitchen island. So I laughed, hoping to bluff my way through; a sitcom, a new take on the Odd Couple.

Exiled. One arm stiffly pointing in the direction of the Pacific Ocean she summed up her aggravations in one word: *barbarian*.

Up ahead on the left was my morning's destination, a modern, two-story, yellow stucco building with purposely protruding i-beams. It housed the Peach Cat & Dog Hospital and heralded the gentrification of funky Venice. I parked in back and got out.

The thing was this: Kiyoko believed all human suffering sprang from the denial of death. That denial took the form of greed, anger, and foolishness. And I agreed. Hell, I couldn't agree more. But before everybody wised up there'd be problems here and there. That's my line. My name's Dick Henry. They call me the Shortcut Man.

Clark Peach, wringing his hands, met me at the back door. Clark was five foot seven, weighed all of a hundred and twenty pounds, peered at the world through delicate gold-rimmed spectacles. He was one of the premier veterinarians in Los Angeles, according to a magazine that evaluated stuff like that. Ferocious, intractable beasts become docile in his presence. I'd seen that. But people? People were a different kind of beast.

"Thanks for coming, Dick."

I liked him a lot. He'd actually done something useful with his life. "You the man, Dr. Peach," I slanged. "Whazzup?"

Of course, I had a good idea what was up.

Dr. Peach kicked an invisible piece of dirt on the floor, then looked up. "Uh, he's, uh, he's back."

I nodded. Dr. Peach was at the butt end of a low-level extortion scam perpetrated by Loman London.

I'd told London to go away early last week. "I didn't see him on my way in, Doc."

Dr. Peach checked his watch. "He'll be here anytime now."

"Why didn't you call me sooner?"

The doctor shrugged, with a tinge of embarrassment. "I, uh, I thought maybe I could talk to him myself."

Hence my vocation.

Doc Peach beckoned to me to follow him. He walked into his office, looked out through the blinds. He turned to me, nodded.

I took a look for myself.

Loman London was a fiftyish wastrel whose contributions to society had not yet added up to a popcorn fart. Two hundred seventy or so pounds were apportioned over his large frame with a hefty surplus accumulating at the waistline. Matted dreadlocks depended thickly to his shoulders. His skin was rough and permanently reddened. Treelike legs, in shorts, interfaced the pavement through a pair of huaraches.

Loman's scam was a simple one. He would set up his rolling incense cart in front of a likely business and wait to be paid to go somewhere else. In the meantime he would frighten the little blue-haired old ladies bringing their little blue poodles in for a checkup.

I turned to the doc. "I guess Mr. London has a learning disability. I'll go out and have a talk with him."

But first I retrieved an accelerant from the Caddy's trunk. I walked around the building. Tendrils of pungent smoke rose from the incense stand into the morning air. I actually liked the smell. Rastaman greeted me in friendly fashion.

"Salutations, mon. What's your pleasure? Sandalwood or Pondicherry Pine?" Loman spoke in a pseudo-Jamaican patois.

I stared at him for a second. Beneath his sunny innocence was a surly streak. "I thought we discussed this, pal. You were going to exhibit elsewhere."

"And I did, mon. That was last week. This is this week."

The "mon" shit irritated me all over again. Loman the lump hadn't been within a thousand miles of Jamaica. Though I was sure he'd smoked ten thousand spliffs. On someone else's dime.

"Doctor Peach isn't going to pay you again. He asks that you move on."

There I was. The soul of reason. Even though I had just begun to feel that peculiar tingling in my fists.

Rastaman shrugged. "And I have entertained his request, mon. Dr. Peach a good mon. But I have found a home for my business. This is a free country, mon."

"The doctor patiently asks you to move on."

Rastaman shrugged with hint of brusqueness. "I have found a home for my business, mon."

"And you refuse to listen to reason." I was giving bad Bob Marley a last chance. I imagined the I-Three's shaking their heads in unison behind him. Of course, London wasn't appreciating his opportunity.

"I refuse to be intimidated, if that's what you mean, mon."

He folded his thick arms over his thick chest. His friendliness had evaporated.

His chin was calling to my knuckles, but, thinking of Kiyoko, I hung on a little longer. "I guess you don't recognize the former light-heavyweight champion of the Thirteenth Naval District."

"Should I be worried, mon?"

It was the "mon" that did it. I stepped around his wares, planted my left foot, launched a right uppercut. The karma missile caught him on the point of the chin and set him, with a thud, flatly on his ass, knocking the wind out of him.

I reached into my back pocket for the can of Ronsonol Lighter Fluid and soaked down the entire incense stand.

Rastaman had not yet regained his feet. He shook his head as if to clear it.

Having survived some righteous shots both in and out of the ring, I knew what he was experiencing. He was hearing a great swarm of bees, though he could not see them.

I indicated his stand. "You ever get your shnozz into what these things smell like when they're all burning at once?"

I patted down my pockets with a theatrical flair. Had I really forgotten my lighter?

Awareness slowly crept into Rastaman's face. He looked at his incense stand, then the yellow Ronsonol can.

"Does anyone have a match around here?" I laid my request before the universe.

Rastaman held up a belaying hand.

But the universe had seen fit to reply.

"I got a match, brother."

My heart warmed. I turned and there was Rojas, right on schedule. "Enrique Montalvo Rojas! As I live and breathe!"

Artfully chapeaued in black porkpie, Enrique Rojas was a badass Eastsider. An old colleague with a supremely checkered past, he had romanced heroin, done a stretch at San Quentin, and had found a cat's eye worth a million dollars in Sri Lanka that currently supported an orphanage or two. He bore a passionate love for Eric Dolphy and Thelonius Monk. "Epistrophy," baby.

Rojas eyed the stand. "Should I light it on fire?"

I smiled. "Please."

From the sidewalk Rastaman waved his hand. "Whoah, now. That's my entire stock, there, man." Man, not *mon*.

I indicated Rojas. "This is Señor Rojas. Señor Rojas loves to beat the shit out of white fools with dreadlocks. Especially ones trying to shake down veterinarians in Venice. Have I made myself clear?"

Rastaman now grasped the full breadth of his misapprehension. "I get it, man. Real clear. Don't burn my shit. I got places to go. Please."

Rojas lit a match. "Shall we give the dude another chance?"

"*Please*," begged Loman the lump.

I feigned consideration.

"*One* more chance?" queried Rojas again, appearing for a second to be a nice guy.

"Uhhh . . ." I watched London hang on my every word. ". . . uhh, nah." I shook my head. "Light him up."

"Okay," said Rojas, bubbling with good cheer. He tossed the match onto the stand and it went up in a huge whoosh of flame and wave of heat.

"Thank you, Señor Rojas." I bowed low.

"Thank you, Señor Henry." Rojas bowed in return.